KEEPER OF THE WATCH

DIMENSION 7 – BOOK 1

KRISTEN L JACKSON

BLACK ROSE writing™

The final approval for this literary material is granted by the author.

Second printing

This is a work of fiction. Names, characters, businesses, places, events and incidents are either the products of the author's imagination or used in a fictitious manner. Any resemblance to actual persons, living or dead, or actual events is purely coincidental.

ISBN: 978-1-61296-981-7
PUBLISHED BY BLACK ROSE WRITING
www.blackrosewriting.com

Printed in the United States of America
Suggested Retail Price (SRP) $18.95

Keeper of the Watch is printed in Gentium Book Basic

DEDICATIONS:

For my Dad, who passed his love of watches and time on to me. You were the inspiration for this story. This one's for you, Dad! Love you!

With love to my husband, Glenn, for letting me bounce ideas off of him at all hours of the day while I am immersed in the writing process, and to my sons Jordan and Jeremy for encouraging me to never give up, even when I wanted to- I love you guys!

I want to thank the following people for their help and encouragement through the entire writing process:

-to my alpha reader and husband, Glenn, for helping during the creation process. The flag in Dimension 7 wouldn't exist without your input (as well as other additions to the story I'm sure!)

-to Mom, Kelley, and Michele for beta reading, love, and support!

-to my friends John Vance and Victoria A Wilder for beta reading and providing the cover blurbs. I truly can't thank you enough!

-to Laura of Laura Danielle Photography for my very professional author photos.

-to Fiction-Atlas Press and Courtney Cannon for copy-editing services.

-to Reagan Rothe and Black Rose Writing for believing in my story, and David King for the amazing cover art.

-and finally, to all of my friends and family who have been so supportive through this entire journey. This book wouldn't exist without all of you! Thank you, thank you, thank you! XOXO

KEEPER OF
THE WATCH

CHAPTER I

The first time Chase saw the watch, he thought it was junk. Just an old, broken thing to be tossed aside. With all the recent advances in technology, he had no need for an outdated watch like this one. As he continued sorting through his recently departed Uncle Charlie's belongings he dismissed the wristwatch, having every intention of throwing it away.

While preparing to leave, Chase reached a hand toward the old timepiece and a sudden electrical charge filled the air. The entire room seemed to sizzle and shake as if an earthquake had struck, and he grabbed onto his uncle's desk chair as the air around him hummed with an unknown power. When his fingers made contact with the watch, a jolt traveled from his fingertips to his toes, making the hair on his arms and legs stand on end. His blood came alive inside his body; pulsing, writhing, wanting ... and he felt a powerful magnetic pull toward the watch.

What the...? He jerked back abruptly, sucking his injured fingers, little pinpricks still racing inside their tips where they had touched the watch.

Stupid watch. Why had Uncle Charlie kept this old thing? In all the years of living with his uncle, Chase couldn't recall ever seeing him wear it. And why had he kept it in the safe locked away with all of his valuables? *It can't be worth anything. It doesn't even work.*

It must have some sentimental value only known to Charlie. Chase would probably never know what made this watch special in the eyes of his crazy old uncle. But for some reason, unknown even to him, when he reached for the watch again, he found himself placing it safely inside his pocket instead of tossing it into the junk pile as he had intended. No magical or mysterious electricity filled the air on the second contact with the thing.

Must've been a static shock, probably caused by friction. With one decisive headshake, he flipped the lightswitch and turned to leave. His imagination was running away with him.

Again.

CHAPTER 2

Picking up his pace, Chase fought the urge to look over his shoulder. *I'm losing it. Why would anyone follow me?* He shook his head and took a deep breath. He hadn't seen anything the last time he'd turned around, or the ten times before that.

But he was almost certain someone *was* following him. Chase continued walking along the waterfront, heading toward work. His temporary summer job was located on the water, and that was the one redeeming quality about scooping ice cream at By the Scoop. *Well, besides meeting all the hot girls.* There were always plenty of lonely girls, vacationing with their families and just looking to break away to spend time with the local boy. He'd always been more than happy to be that guy. Until recently.

Without even being aware he was doing it, he scanned the crowd as he walked along. *No one is following me. I'm just being paranoid.* And yet he gave in to the tickle at the back of his neck and stole yet another glance over his shoulder, again not seeing anyone, or anything that seemed out of place. Still, he couldn't shake the fingers of dread that crawled up his spine as he walked. This wasn't the first time he had felt this way. Ever since his eighteenth birthday, three weeks ago, he'd often caught himself looking over his shoulder in search of something, or someone. Lately, every sound made him jump; every person made him wary. Was he being followed? That just seemed crazy. Usually, Chase was over-confident in every aspect of his life. These new bouts of paranoia were an anomaly.

Nonetheless, he briskly walked along, resisting the urge to look back yet again, missing the heavy beat of hard rock music that usually pounded in his ears. He'd abandoned this habit in recent weeks to pay closer attention to his surroundings, just in case. *In case ... what?* Chase shook his head. He yearned for the soothing chaos the music provided him. Music had always been an escape for him. He looked longingly out over the shimmering waves, the evening light mystically refracting off the water. The cathartic ebb and flow of the waves were another. He breathed deep, savoring the salty smell, wishing he could ditch work and go swimming. Shoulders slumped, he sighed and moved on.

In his distracted state, he bumped into a passerby and lurched backward, arms raised in automatic defense. His heart beat a fierce rhythm as he braced for, and even welcomed, the anticipated fight with all the pent-up energy of the past few weeks. *Let's do this.*

"Hey, Chase! How's it goin'?" the person asked, as he enthusiastically pounded Chase on the back.

Willing the stiffness out of his stance, Chase recognized his classmate and replied, "Oh, hey Brian. On my way to work. What's up with you?"

"Packin' for college. I'll be heading out in three weeks. I'm stoked, man. Are you packed? What university are you attending? You won that football scholarship, right? I can't remember where you..."

"I ... don't know if I'm going to college. I'm taking a year to decide. That's great, Brian. It was nice to see you. I miss seeing everyone since graduation. We should get the gang together before everyone leaves. I'll talk to Mason about it."

"Yeah, man. Great idea!" Brian turned to leave, and hesitated. "Hey, Chase. I heard about your uncle, but I was away when it happened. I'm sorry, man. He was always nice to me."

"Thanks, Bri."

"See you, man."

With long strides, Chase continued on his way, mentally rehashing that last crucial football game. He shook his head and clenched his jaw as he relived the game yet again. *Why didn't I catch that ball?* That mistake had cost him the scholarship. And now he'd lost Uncle Charlie. 'The Game' didn't seem as important after that. His inner voice whispered, *You were never sure about football as a career, anyway...* but Uncle Charlie had been so proud.

Still, it was good to see Brian. At least it had been a distraction from his recent paranoia.

· · ·

He arrived at work safely, tied on his apron, and got busy. This was peak season, so the place was always full of vacationers looking for a cool treat to alleviate the heat of the day. He juggled taking orders, preparing them, and cashiering while keeping up a steady banter with the customers. With his tall, good looks and his sun-streaked blond hair, he had never had to work very hard at getting a date. Girls melted when he flashed his dimples, and despite his recent melancholy tonight was no different. One girl in particular hung around the shop for much longer than it took to eat her single scoop cone. Before she left, she wrote her phone number on a napkin, and winked shyly as she handed it to him. Ava. What a nice name to go along with those big, green eyes and long, vacation-tanned legs. *Just the kind of distraction I need.* The interaction gave him back a small measure of normalcy, and his heart lightened in his chest for the first time in weeks.

At the end of his shift, with the late evening breeze coming off the water, he clocked out and exited through the back door instead of the front. He knew he was letting his paranoia take over, but if anyone was out there waiting for him they wouldn't be expecting him to leave through the back door.

Not for the first time, he wished he owned a car. The house was only ten blocks away, but in his current state, he thought driving the ten blocks would be preferable. Technically, now that Uncle Charlie was gone, he supposed he did own a car. If you could call that old clunker a car. Uncle Charlie sure had loved that ancient piece of junk. He could picture it now, his uncle lovingly calling it "a classic" as he polished the faded olive-green paint. As much as he had loved his crazy, eccentric uncle, he had to draw the line somewhere. *No way am I taking Ava out in that ugly old thing.* No rational, sane girl would be impressed to be driving around in the beat up 1974 AMC Gremlin. Luckily he didn't need a car, since everything around here was conveniently located for the tourists. If he and Ava ever did go out, they would just have to walk.

Chase's head darted from side to side as he rushed home, trying to take in everything and pay attention to details. Nothing looked suspicious or out of place, and he didn't get the strange sensation of being watched on his way. He arrived at Uncle Charlie's house—his house now—and reached out to put the key into the keyhole.

As he turned the key, smoke began rising from inside his pocket, great billowing puffs of gray smog from within. The electric shock vibrated through his hip and traveled up his body. Chase clutched at his hip and remembered the watch he had placed there that morning. He tore the thing out of his pocket, and though it was hot to the touch, surprisingly it didn't burn him. It was an unfamiliar kind of heat, and he felt drawn toward it. He did not have an urge to drop it on contact, instead, he irrationally wanted to get as close as he could. It was almost ... welcoming. It beckoned him. His left wrist began to ache, and he once again felt the magnetic pull of his body toward the watch. It was as if it needed him to put it on, and his body reciprocated that need. As before, he could feel every cell of his blood as it flowed in his veins and pumped through his beating heart in a mesmerizing *swish-swish swish-swish*, which kept a perfect rhythm to match the ticking hands of the watch. In that moment, his body came to life as it never had before, and his mind went blank except for this one all-consuming connection. He reached out for the watchband ...

A large *CRASH* broke the silence of the night. It had come from somewhere inside the house. All of his energy had been focused solely on the watch, and the noise instantly jerked him out of his trance. He jammed the watch back into his pocket, pulled out his cell phone, and dialed 911 as he turned the key and opened the door. He didn't think about what he was doing, instead let instinct take over and rushed into the house yelling, "Who's there?" to the room in general.

Looking slowly around the room, he found the source of the sound. A lamp lay on the floor next to the table, shade askew, and he picked it up and held it defensively like a baseball bat above his head. As the minutes ticked by his shoulders began to relax, and he lowered the light and replaced it on the table, reaching around to plug it in. The silence of the house was eerie, and he reached down to wipe his palms on his pants as his eyes searched every dark corner. He flipped the lightswitch just as the sound of a door slamming echoed through the house, and bounded across the room in time to see the door bounce back open, straining on its hinges as it banged loudly against the kitchen wall like a gunshot. When he looked outside, he couldn't see anyone in the inky blackness. *Should I follow?*

His body lurched at the sound of a knock on the front door. "Police!"

Inhaling deeply, he let them in. As the two patrolmen entered through the front door, he bellowed, "He went out the back door!" pointing in the direction of the kitchen. Without a word, they jogged out the back and disappeared into the blackness of night. In the silence that followed, Chase wandered through the house, careful not to touch anything else. He had seen enough CSI episodes to have a good idea of what would happen when the officers returned.

For the millionth time in the past three weeks, he wished Uncle Charlie were here to lighten the mood. Chase flopped down on the couch and leaned his head back as he let the memories come. His uncle had a way of making the people around him laugh at the most inopportune moments. Chase could hear the sound of his laughter as clearly as if he were sitting right next to him. He would chuckle through the telling of a joke, barely able to contain his joy before the ending, and then boisterously laugh until tears came to his eyes as he slapped his hip as though he couldn't handle the hilarity. No one else would understand the punch line, but inevitably they would laugh with him just because his laughter was contagious. He really did miss that old man.

When the officers returned, they were alone. After searching the house room by room, they came back to the living room.

"There's no sign of forced entry, and everything is in place. Did you see anything or anyone?"

Chase shook his head as he answered, "No. I heard a noise before I came in, and the lamp was on the floor. Then I heard the kitchen door bang."

The two officers looked at each other over his head. The taller one nodded.

"Maybe you left the door unlatched this morning. You probably didn't realize it was open, and your imagination created a thief in the house," concluded the tall, thin, obviously rookie cop. "Possibly the lamp was near the edge of the table, and it fell off?" He didn't look much older than Chase. *What does he know?*

"Even though this time it was a false alarm, make sure you lock all of your doors tonight. Next time, it could be the real deal." Advised the shorter, pudgier officer. He looked like he had stopped at one too many donut shops recently. No wonder the intruder had gotten away.

Thanks for the help, guys. I would never have thought of locking the doors tonight, he thought sarcastically. *They don't believe me because I'm a teenager.* Eighteen. Legally an adult, but no one actually treats you that way.

His uncle had instilled in him the need for security from a very young age, even taking him to target practice at the age of eight. He could shoot a gun in his sleep and still hit the bullseye, dead center. He would never go to sleep without locking all the doors, and the windows, too. Chase took a deep breath and crossed his arms in front of his chest.

I'm sure I heard someone in the house. It wasn't my imagination. Was it? Chase began to question himself. He knew he hadn't opened the back door at all today. So that meant he hadn't left it open or even unlocked. What explanation was there other than an intruder in the house? *I didn't actually see anything, and I was distracted by that stupid watch... Maybe I'm just tired. It has been a long day. Maybe after I get some sleep, I'll be able to think more rationally. Like an adult.* Chase grumbled as he moved through the house.

He yanked the watch out of his pocket and put it in the top drawer of the end table in the living room, slamming it shut with bang that echoed through the empty house. This time, it did not feel hot to the touch, nor did his body strain toward it. Yes, lack of sleep was the culprit. *Either that, or I'm losing my mind.* He dragged his feet up the stairs to his bedroom, pausing briefly on his way past Uncle Charlie's room. *I really do miss you, old man.* The sting of unshed tears burned behind his eyes, and he blinked them back.

Uncle Charlie's words flashed through his memory, "Next to laughter, sleep is the best medicine in this world." Chase had always suspected that he had made that up to excuse his frequent napping, but maybe the saying had some merit after all. Chase hadn't been getting enough sleep lately; that was all. His uncle had always attributed his own good health to the daily naps he'd enjoyed.

His good health had run out, though, hadn't it? Chase turned out the light and suffered through yet another restless night.

CHAPTER 3

The intruders, a man, and a woman, were furious and frustrated. They were dressed all in black, which blended well with their midnight hair. Though they were not related, they looked as if they could be siblings with their tall, lean build and dark eyes to match their hair. The woman paced the small room. Back and forth, back and forth.

"We have to find that watch and destroy it!" she snarled.

Their lives depended on it. The attempt to find it inside the house had been a failure. They had looked through every inch of that place, but they were professionals, and she was positive that no sign of their presence had been left behind. Except the lamp. *Stupid mistake.* Her eyes narrowed on the man.

They'd escaped the house just in time. The pair had watched those silly cops running around in the dark from their carefully concealed hiding place right under the officer's noses. When they didn't want to be seen, they had ways of becoming virtually invisible.

"Where would that crazy old man hide it?" hissed the woman.

"How should I know? You're the one that insisted we break into the house. I say we just grab the boy and make him tell us. He has to know about it by now. He turned eighteen three weeks ago, so the process has already begun. He doesn't have to get hurt if he hands over the watch," growled her companion.

They had been following the boy, Chase Walker, since his birthday, looking for signs of The Coupling. He had not been wearing the watch earlier this evening, so maybe there was still time.

She reluctantly nodded in acknowledgment. Secrecy was essential to their mission, but so was the acquisition of Chase's watch, and all others like it. There were only three watches left in existence. All others had been destroyed. She would do whatever she had to in order to end the power of the watches once and for all. Even if it meant killing the boy. She didn't enjoy murder, but she had done it before as a last resort, and she would do what she must to guarantee her success. She truly believed the existence of everyone in this world, and others, hinged on her victory.

"Grab him at the next opportunity," she called over her shoulder as she stomped out of the room.

CHAPTER 4

Alyx was hunting the hunters. She watched the man and the woman leave the house, and followed them to a run-down hotel off the highway. They had no idea she currently resided in this dimension, even if it would only be until 7:07 on July 7th. She had the element of surprise on her side. That didn't give her much time to reach her goal before she would have to jump to the next dimension.

If they knew she was here, right under their noses, they would hunt her even more ruthlessly than they now hunted the new keeper of the watch. He hadn't even coupled with his watch yet. She had to protect him from the watch hunters.

Her parents had prepared her for this for as long as she could remember. It was her destiny. They had trained her well in self-defense, and she excelled in many fields of combat. She was a girl who could definitely take care of herself, and now it was her responsibility to take care of this new keeper, as well.

Alyx glanced at her own watch, now an extension of her body, as it had been since just after her eighteenth birthday three months ago. The watch glowed purple in the darkness. She felt such a strong connection with it as if the watch shared her emotions, and her very soul, as well as her bloodline.

She observed as the woman slammed out the door and stomped to her car. The woman did not like failure, and she had failed tonight. Alyx knew she would stop at nothing to destroy all remaining watches. Her people had always hunted them. The hunters. Just as Alyx's family had always protected them. The keepers. Both near the brink of extinction, fighting now for their very existence.

Alyx had a decision to make. Follow the woman, or stay with the man? After a moment of thought, she decided to stay with the man. The woman often sent him to do her dirty work, so she was banking on the man going after the new keeper. They probably hoped to retrieve and destroy the watch before the boy even had a chance to initiate The Coupling. Alyx planned to be there to stop them. Her sole purpose for being in this dimension out of schedule was to make sure that the boy and the watch made that ultimate connection. Her family had risked much to make this happen, and she would not fail them now.

CHAPTER 5

A week after finding the watch, Chase awoke with a start, heart pounding and clothing soaked through. He had dreamed of the watch. In his dream, it was speaking to him, though not with words. Telepathically. The watch wanted him to put it on. He shook his head to clear out the cobwebs as he stumbled to the bathroom. This was absurd. *I'm never wearing that thing.* He had to figure out what to do with it. Obviously, he couldn't keep it here, so maybe he'd drop by the pawn shop on Tenth Street tonight before work to unload it. That watch was starting to creep him out.

He was scheduled to work the night shift again, and since he had the entire day to kill, Chase decided to head to the beach. He hadn't done that since his uncle had died exactly one week before his birthday, and he knew he would feel better when his feet hit the sand. He took his phone out of his pocket and sent a quick text to Mason.

Sunset Beach @ 10?

He hadn't seen his friend since graduation, and he'd missed him since school had ended.

Mason's response was almost immediate.

C U there.

On the way out the door, he noticed his recently widowed, elderly neighbor unloading bags of groceries from her car. Though he wasn't really in the mood, he jogged over to help. Mentally sighing, as he took the bag from her hand and two more from the car, he said: "Mrs. Ruiz, you know you can call me anytime you need help."

"I know I can, Chase. You're such a nice boy. Your uncle would be proud. He was proud," she said, pinching his cheek as if he were five years old. She would always think of him as a little boy. "I don't want to be a bother. You already do all my yard work at no charge."

"You're never a bother, Mrs. Ruiz. Is there anything else you need done while I'm here? I'm on my way to the beach, but I have a few minutes," he asked, mentally groaning. Mason was waiting for him.

"Well, now that you mention it if you really don't mind...."

•   •   •

He arrived at the beach to find Mason already there. No explanation was needed for his tardiness. His friend knew him well enough to know that if he arrived late, there must be a good reason.

Mason jogged over and punched him in the arm. "Bout time. I been watchin' this volleyball competition. We can smoke 'em. You in?"

"You know it." They offered to challenge the winners of the current game.

They'd always made a good team, even though they didn't agree on much of anything. They were opposites, even in looks. While Chase was six feet tall and muscular in a lean sort of way, Mason was a good six inches shorter, and though not fat, he could stand to lose fifteen pounds. Chase was blond with blue eyes; Mason had red hair and freckles. Mason preferred a video game controller and Chase went for outdoor sports, but somehow it worked anyway. The two had met in second grade and had been best buds ever since.

As predicted, they crushed the other team and collapsed on the sand, sweat glistening and chests heaving.

Just as he was cracking open a can of Coke, little fingers of apprehension crawled up his spine as he once again had the feeling of being watched. He casually looked all around him, trying to pinpoint the source of this now-familiar suspicion. Mason, knowing him so well, immediately picked up on his mood.

"What's up, bro?" was all he needed to say to get Chase to spill everything that had been happening lately. He told him about finding the watch and how his body reacted to it, about the feeling of being followed, and about the break-in at the house last night. As always, his friend sat quietly and listened.

"Why don't you come stay with me for a while? You know my parents love you, man. They won't mind." Leave it to Mason to just casually accept this crazy story without wanting to put him in the psych ward. His eyes burned with emotion, and he gulped it back. Mason was getting ready to move out of state to begin his first year of college in the fall. Chase was going to miss him when he moved away. Everything was changing, and he was feeling nostalgic for the days of his youth now that he was officially a legal adult. He didn't feel any different, but suddenly because he was 'eighteen,' he was supposed to know everything, even though he still felt like a kid on the inside. He had no idea where he should go from here.

"Thanks, but I really think I need to work this through. And I don't want to leave Uncle Charlie's house empty after the break in. I'll be fine, but I appreciate the offer, Mace." Chase slapped Mason on the back as he spoke.

They left the beach, each heading their separate ways. Chase did feel better after a day of sun, sand, and male bonding. He always had. The beach always seemed to have a soothing effect on his soul, and being with Mason had helped, too.

Still, he carefully surveilled the area, taking in small details he normally would not notice as he ambled along. The woman on the beach towel across from him reading the same book he had read last year, the man in the speedo jogging on the beach, the couple digging in the sand with their two children, a man with midnight black hair standing off in the distance who seemed to be people watching. Everything he saw appeared to be a normal beach activity. Nothing to raise his suspicions. And yet ... he shivered as if icicles traveled down his spine. *Something is wrong.* The feeling stayed with him all the way home. *I really am losing my mind.* No one was following him, he was sure of it.

As he slowly opened the front door, Chase tilted his head to listen for any sound coming from inside. When silence was his only answer, he stepped in and shut the door, sliding the deadbolt home with a bang. He leaned back against the wood for just a second, then pushed himself up and went upstairs to prepare for his shift.

CHAPTER 6

While Chase had been enjoying his day at the beach, Alyx was making preparations. She carried various weapons from this world and others in her purple backpack, making an effort to blend in with other girls her age who were preparing to attend college. If she made it through her eighteenth year, she would attend college back in her home dimension too. Like a normal eighteen-year-old. She already knew she would choose to stay in her home dimension when her year ended on her nineteenth birthday, April 4th at 4:04. Her time to make the choice.

All keepers knew the risks involved in jumping. The hunters were always there, in each dimension, working toward the extinction of the watches and their keepers. She accepted it. Though she didn't want to die, she would, if she must, to protect her family's legacy.

Her mind snapped back to the present. The man had spied on the new keeper all day at the beach, trying to blend in. To her, it was obvious he wasn't just enjoying a day at the beach, but the new keeper hadn't seemed aware of the danger lurking right behind him. *I'll have to train him better than that if he is to survive his year of jumping.*

His watch would help once they coupled, too. The watches could sense when a hunter was near, and that was how Alyx was following the man. She could not sense the woman nearby, and a shiver of apprehension crawled down her neck as she wondered what she was up to.

Just then, Chase walked out onto his porch and began walking, and she watched as the man followed at a distance. Vacationers were swarming the waterfront like ants on an anthill at this time of evening, so Alyx did not worry that he would try to take the new keeper right now.

Even so, as the man followed the boy, she followed the man. She couldn't take the chance that the hunter would break his people's number one rule ... secrecy. They were getting desperate lately. There were two hunters in each dimension, a man and a woman. Well, technically, they were the same man and woman in each dimension. It was their 'other selves' that resided in the alternate worlds.

With three watches left, the keepers were outnumbered. That's why it was imperative that she and the new keeper stick together as much as they could. Her family had worked long and hard to guarantee that they would be in the same dimensions at the same times, at least until she turned nineteen and her year ended. The new keeper would be on his own for his last month of jumping, but hopefully, he would have learned enough to keep himself alive by then.

The date is July first. Six days left to achieve her goal. She had to get the new keeper to couple with his watch as soon as possible before the jump. The plan had been to let him do it in his own time, but they didn't have the luxury of time anymore. Alyx decided that she would have to kick-start The Coupling herself, since the boy didn't seem to know how to do it on his own, despite the pull of the watch itself. If he was resisting the watch's pull, this boy must have a very strong will. The watches were very insistent. After all, they can remain dormant for years as they wait for the next keeper in the bloodline. The watch would help. That gave her encouragement in her quest as she continued to follow the hunter.

She made a sound of disgust and rolled her eyes as she witnessed the boy flirting across the counter with a suntanned beauty that flirted back relentlessly. She felt an instant dislike of this girl, though she didn't know why.

We don't have time for this, she fumed. Her cheeks burned and she clenched her hands, then took a slow deep breath and willed her hands to relax. *Why should I care if he flirts with ten girls?* Her only mission was to witness the coupling and keep him alive for his year of jumping to ensure the continuation of the keeper's legacy. She had no other interest in this boy.

CHAPTER 7

Chase felt his sanity waning like the tide. All night at work, his eyes darted back and forth and he looked at everyone who came through the door with suspicion. He couldn't shake the familiar feeling of being watched. Maybe tomorrow he should go check himself into the looney bin. He was starting to believe that he really was losing his mind.

Even when Ava stopped in, ordering a double scoop of cookies and cream, he was barely able to pay attention. *What is wrong with me?* Still, they set a date to go jet skiing the next day, and that would give him a welcome distraction from all the craziness that had been in his life for the past few weeks. After Ava left, the evening shift seemed to drag.

As he left work, again through the back door, a sudden urgency to be home consumed him, and he felt his body pick up speed until he was full-out running. His sneakers pounded a steady rhythm on the sidewalk, and he wiped the sweat from his eyes with the back of his hand. His paranoia took over and he did not go directly home, instead choosing a more circuitous route. He knew he was acting crazy, but at this moment, he didn't care. Sweat soaked his shirt, but still, he ran.

He burst through the front door and slammed it behind him so hard the frame shook. Only when he was safely standing in his living room, the locked door at his back, did his body start to lose its tension. Until a new threat broke through his relief. *What's that smell? Is that a ... a ... burning smell?* His nostrils flared as fumes stung. *Is the house on fire?*

Chase bounded up the stairs, taking two at a time, and stopped in each room. When he found nothing, he ran downstairs to discover the living room now filled with smoke. It stung his eyes, and he waved his hands in front of his face to clear the way. *Where is it coming from?* Chase's head darted in every direction trying to locate the source. It seemed to be coming from ... the end table drawer. The watch. He realized he had forgotten to get rid of the thing this afternoon. A hum of electricity filled the air, and the table began to rock back and forth on its legs as if it had come to life. Suddenly, the drawer burst open, and the watch flew out. It landed, vibrating on the floor at his feet, and he jumped back.

"No no no no," he chanted, taking another step back.

As before, Chase felt a strong pull toward the watch. It was happening again. He had promised himself he would not wear the watch, and he meant to keep that pledge. Even though every nerve in his body seemed to strain toward the thing, he resisted the pull. It took all his willpower to deny this powerful need that consumed him and turn away from it as he ran down to the basement to find something to put the watch into until he could get rid of it. He found a metal toolbox, dumped the contents on the floor, and bounded back up the stairs.

As he slowly approached the watch, he felt words form inside his head. They were not his words. They belonged to another. He put his hands over his ears, body hunched forward, fighting the words even as he heard them echo through his brain.

This is your destiny. Do not resist your destiny. We are one. Do not resist it. We need each other. Please. We are one.

Crap. He was hearing voices in his head now. His fears were confirmed; he *had* lost his mind. At least his alter ego was polite. Please. Ha! He would have thought if he were going to have another personality, it would be a tough, kick-ass, other self. It might have said, "Put the watch on, NOW!" Maybe then he would have listened.

Instead, Chase grabbed the watch, threw it into the toolbox, and slammed the lid with a decisive *bang*. The box was fireproof, so he didn't need to worry about it catching fire. Just in case, he placed the toolbox into the freezer and shut the door with a thud.

CHAPTER 8

Scrape.

Chase raised his head off the pillow, heart skipping in his chest. He'd heard a sound coming from downstairs. Since he hadn't actually been sleeping, the small scraping sound carried up the stairs, and his body instantly went on full alert. He quietly reached into his nightstand, removing the old .45 caliber handgun he had been keeping in his bedroom since his uncle's death. It was already loaded, and he flipped off the safety as he inched out of bed. The weapon felt familiar in his hands. It ought to. He and his uncle had been visiting the shooting range since he was a boy. Creeping through the doorway Chase straightened, coming to a decision. He was going to end this once and for all.

He crept down the hall, avoiding the familiar creaky floorboards, and snuck down the stairs. When he reached the living room he paused, tilting his head. His nighttime eyes were already adjusted to the darkness, but he could neither see, nor hear anything out of place. The moonlight shining in through the front window gave off just enough light so that he could remain hidden, while still observing the room. He crouched down behind the recliner clutching the gun, and waited. He could be patient when he needed to be.

He tilted his head once again. The only sound was the steady *tick-tick-tick* of the clock in the dining room ... and silence. His legs began to cramp, and feelings of self-doubt invaded his brain. *Maybe the sound I heard was just the house settling.* He couldn't remember ever hearing that particular sound before tonight, but then again, he had never been as jumpy before, either. Shoulders slumped, he began to relax, and felt for the safety on his weapon to flip it back on. He should go back to bed and try to at least get in a few hours of sleep tonight. Despite having that thought, some innate instinct made him remain in his hiding spot behind the chair just a bit longer.

If it hadn't been so quiet in the house, and he on high alert, Chase probably would not have noticed the minuscule sound of the basement doorknob turning ever so slowly. Though his heart pounded a million beats per minute, he stayed in his hiding spot and prayed that the sound of his shallow breathing would not give him away. *Who could it be? How long has he or she been hiding in my basement?* Chase had no answers. He felt a drop of cold sweat trickle into his eye but didn't dare raise his hand to wipe it. All he knew was that this person was here to do harm. He could sense it.

The intruder was now in the living room, heading toward the stairs, walking ever so slowly to remain anonymous. Luckily, it seemed he did not notice Chase just a few feet away behind the chair. Slowly, the man, he was almost positive it was a man, crept up the stairs. *What does he want with me?*

Chase knew when the man arrived at his destination, he would find an empty bed and realize his target was somewhere else in the house. He had two choices. Run upstairs and confront him, or go out the front door right now, which seemed the logical thing to do. But then this charade would continue, and Chase was ready for it to end, one way or the other. *And what if there is more than one intruder in the house right now?*

He had never been a coward, and he wouldn't start now. Uncle Charlie had taught him better than that. Decision made, he flipped the safety off for the second time, made a move to stand, and felt arms grab at him from behind. *How did he get behind me?* Chase wondered fleetingly before self-preservation kicked in and he instictually grabbed the arm that restrained him. Springing to action, he thrust his elbow backward into the person holding him and heard a whoosh as air was expelled. He heard a frantic voice whisper in his ear "I'm here to help. That man upstairs is here to kill you. Where is the watch?"

The watch? What did the watch have to do with this? "I don't know what watch you're talking about," Chase whispered back.

His arm burned as it was twisted behind his back, and he felt the tickle of breath on his ear as a voice hissed, "We don't have time for this. I'll explain later, but right now we have to go! I'm on your side. Where. Is. The. Watch?"

In a split second, he made a decision to believe this stranger. Maybe it was because he had just seen a man sneak up his stairs toward the place he was supposed to be fast asleep to do who-knows-what, but he felt as if a little help would be appreciated at this point.

"Okay. Let go. It's in the kitchen, this way." Chase led the stranger to the kitchen, opened the freezer, and took out the toolbox. The girl laid her left hand on the outside of the box, closed her eyes, and for the first time, he noticed she was wearing a watch of her own. It was unlike any he had ever seen, and he sensed an awareness in it similar to the watch that now resided in the metal box. That was where the similarities ended. While his watch looked like an old worn-down relic of times past, hers looked like nothing he had ever seen before. It had a faint ethereal purple glow that surrounded it, but the hands and numbers were a deep blood red. The petite face was octagonal, with what appeared to be brushed chrome edging on it. The thin band was a perfect fit on her wrist. It seemed to pulsate, and as crazy as it sounded, he felt a strange connection to *her* watch.

She opened her eyes, somehow satisfied that his watch was in the toolbox without ever opening the lid, and asked, "Do you have a car?"

Chase hesitated just a second, and then grabbed the keys from the kitchen drawer and pointed in the direction of the garage.

Just then, he jerked his head toward the pounding footsteps on the staircase, and he knew the man had discovered an empty bed upstairs.

"Go start the car. I'll take care of him. You must protect your watch," she furiously whispered as she took off in the direction of the living room.

Chase hesitated. It didn't seem right letting a girl handle this problem by herself. Maybe she would need his help. Instead of heading toward the garage as she had instructed, Chase went back in the direction of the living room. He heard the sounds of combat as flesh met flesh, and entered just as the girl kicked out with her leg, catching the man at the knees and dropping him like an anchor. She pulled a strange looking weapon from her bag, and though Chase had an impressive knowledge-base in weaponry, he had never seen anything like it before. It was shaped similar to a gun but had four metal rings that encircled the barrel, each one smaller than the one before it. When she fired the weapon, it shot off what appeared to be four sparks of light at once. Each spark went its own way, in an uncoordinated circular pattern, toward the man. He had a moment to compare it to fireworks, and then all four sparks made contact simultaneously at four different entry points on the man's body. The intruder went down instantly, his body stiff, either unconscious or dead, he didn't know which.

He froze in the doorway, gun at his side. The whole scene had happened so fast that he hadn't even had time to raise his weapon.

The girl was not pleased that he hadn't done what she told him to.

"Go, now! He wasn't expecting a fight, and he had no idea I was here. Now he knows. We must hurry, she won't be far behind, and she won't be surprised so easily."

She ran past, grabbing his arm, and dragged him to the garage. Chase opened the garage door and uncovered his uncle's car. She didn't react to the hideous vehicle, just grabbed the keys and jumped into the driver's seat.

"I guess you're driving," mumbled Chase as he sat in the passenger seat, toolbox in his lap. "You need to answer some questions. I have a lot of them."

Glancing in his direction, she screeched out of the garage and onto the street as if the man was in hot pursuit instead of immobile in his living room. Though ugly, the Gremlin was a surprisingly powerful piece of machinery.

She gave a slight nod, then ignored him and floored it.

CHAPTER 9

Chase studied the stranger's profile as she drove. In the engulfing darkness, he couldn't make out her face but could see the outline of her shoulder-length straight hair, and petite, if slightly wide, nose. He wasn't sure, but he thought her hair was dark. He wondered what color her eyes were. *Where did that come from?* In light of the events preceding this moment, he was surprised he would even care about something as shallow as eye color. Shaking his head, he turned to stare out the window.

He found himself speechless as he contemplated which question to ask first. None of this made any sense, and he hesitated, wondering if he would like the answers to the questions on the tip of his tongue. After reminding himself that he wasn't a coward, he blurted, "Are you for real?"

She didn't spare him a glance, "Is that really the question you want to ask right now?"

"No, but I can't seem to focus on just one question. Let's start with your name."

"Alyx."

"I should have known you'd have a boy's name, the way you fight. I'm Chase." He answered. "Ok, next. Is the man in my living room dead?"

"No. I mean...probably not."

"So, does that mean he'll be looking for me? If it's the watch he's after. I don't want it ... so he can have it. If I give it to him, will he leave me alone?"

"No. You have a responsibility to protect that watch and its secrets with your life. Besides, the watch will not work for him anyway. It will only work for you. You will feel differently when you put it on."

"No way. I'm never wearing that thing. Next question. Where are we going?"

"I am taking you somewhere private so we can initiate The Coupling," she answered.

Chase's mouth dropped open. "Whoa! Hey, slow down. I know I'm a guy and everything, but we just met. I like to get to know a girl before I get intimate with her." He was annoyed that this stranger had just assumed he'd jump into bed with her. He wasn't that desperate.

"You moron! I would not let you touch me if we were the last man and woman in this dimension! I am not talking about *us*. I am referring to *you* and the *watch* coupling."

Silence followed as Chase's face burned with heat. He wasn't easily embarrassed, but he had been a bit off lately.

"Uh, sorry. You think I'm going to 'couple' with a watch? You're crazy. I mean, thanks for saving my life and everything, but I think we should just go our separate ways. You can keep the watch. I don't want it. It's an ugly old thing anyway. I can't understand what my uncle saw in that old watch, or what makes everyone think it's so special. You don't seem to need me, so..."

She huffed out a breath, "You need to couple with your watch, as all of the chosen relatives in your bloodline have. The watch will allow you to see things that normal people cannot see. To see and to protect. It is your destiny."

"Um. Okay, whatever you say. So, what's the deal with your watch?"

"I celebrated my coupling two days after my eighteenth birthday. I embraced it. You will too, once you accept your fate. The watches are very persuasive. I am surprised you have been able to resist the power for this long. Do not fight it; just give in to the pull of your watch, your destiny. I will explain more when we reach our destination."

Her words rang true, despite his denial. Still, he fought the persuasive energy he could feel coming from inside the metal box as they drove on. Surprisingly, Chase laid his head against the window and slept better than he had in weeks.

CHAPTER 10

When Chase awoke, he was instantly alert. The first thing he saw was a wall of green. He was surrounded by trees. He blinked. They were parked in a small clearing, seemingly in the middle of the woods somewhere. There was a small pop-up tent set up at the far corner near a stream. He did not see any sign of Alyx, and it annoyed him that she had just left him there. Her abandonment sparked a multitude of emotions that warred against each other in an instant. He should just leave the watch here and walk away. *She doesn't need me; she only needs the watch.* He had his own plans, and this girl was interfering in his life. *I didn't ask for any of this.*

He felt an unexpected surge of anger toward his uncle Charlie. Had he known about all of this? The presence of the watch in his safe implied he had. If he'd known, why hadn't he mentioned any of it? All of this would have been easier to accept if he hadn't been left in the dark all these years.

And yet, he found that buried deep underneath all of those emotions, some part of him was missing her. Alyx. Like they were connected, somehow. *Whoa! Connected?* He'd just met her! And she hadn't answered all of his questions yet, anyway. He would stick around just long enough to get answers, and then he was gone.

His sat up straight as he remembered his date with Ava scheduled for this afternoon. He was sorry that he would be a no-show, but he if he was honest with himself, he could admit that he hadn't really been that interested in her anyway. Picturing her standing at the Jet Ski rental shop waiting for him, he felt a twinge of remorse that she would be disappointed. *Should I call her to cancel?* With one quick nod, he reached into his pocket and pulled out his phone. After three rings, Ava picked up.

"Hi Ava, it's Chase. I'm not going to make it today. Something came up. Maybe another time?"

"Oh. Okay. I'm here with my family until the end of the week. If you want, we could go another day before I leave? If you're free?"

"I'll have to get back to you on that."

"Okay. Thanks for calling, Chase."

Chase ended the call and looked up to see Alyx standing two feet away with a look of pure annoyance on her face. This was the first time he was truly seeing her, and he had to struggle to keep his mouth from dropping open. His eyebrows shot up, and his heart picked up its speed.

She stood, hands on her hips, head cocked, and glared. Her shoulder length, dark chocolate hair blew gently in the breeze. Brown did not accurately describe her hair, there were sun-tinted honey colored highlights throughout, while only the hair underneath was dyed purple so that just the tips appeared a deep, dark amethyst color. Her face was round, with high cheekbones giving her a strong appearance. She had a tall, lean, and obviously toned body. He had seen evidence of that. Though not classically beautiful, she was fascinating, and he could not make himself look away. She was dressed in black yoga pants and a purple form-fitting t-shirt with a V-neck, and black and silver sneakers on her feet. The look she was shooting at Chase gave him pause.

And then he really looked at her eyes for the first time. They were an exotic almond shape and were uniquely bluish-violet in color. She had the kind of eyes that draw a person in, though right now they were squinted in anger. Chase had never seen eyes that exact color before, and he felt mesmerized and once again speechless. He thought he could drown in those eyes, so he forced himself to look away. He had never experienced a reaction like this to any girl he had ever met before, and he didn't want to think about the reasons why it was happening with this girl.

"Um. What's up?" he casually asked, wishing he had something more profound to say.

"Who were you talking to? Did you tell her anything? Keeping the secret is imperative, and you are sitting here talking to a *girl*?"

Chase's emotions went from awe to anger in a split second. "Hey, it's none of your business who I talk to. You're just a crazy girl I met yesterday, so back off."

Her watch seemed to pulsate brighter as she spoke, distracting him from his anger. "Why is your watch glowing?"

"I am sick of your questions! I cannot believe you are making a date at a time like this! You need to be thinking about your watch right now, not a girl!" She stomped off into the woods, leaving Chase to fume alone.

Fine. He stomped off in the other direction. What had just happened? Chase didn't know, but he was positive something life-altering had just transpired. He just wasn't sure what.

He walked toward the tent, and decided to take this time to become familiar with his temporary home. Obviously, Alyx had been staying here for some time. There was food, spare clothing ... and weapons. At least he thought they were weapons. Some he recognized and others were foreign to him. He entered the small tent and began taking stock of the arsenal of weapons she had acquired.

A smiled curved his lips. *Now, this might be fun.*

CHAPTER 11

Alyx paced back and forth furiously. How could he make a phone call? To a girl? Didn't he know the danger he was in? That they both were in? Alyx was risking everything to protect both of their watches, and he risked nothing. He never listened to her!

The girl on the phone had probably been the same girl he had flirted with at the ice-cream shop, she fumed. Oh, she had been beautiful, Alyx admitted to herself. And he had noticed, too. She had witnessed other girls checking Chase out, too. Even she could see that he was easy to look at. He was such an interesting person. It was a good thing she didn't care about those things. Though she knew nothing of this girl he had called, she irrationally disliked her for no apparent reason other than ... liking Chase?

Shaking her head, she tilted her head skyward. She didn't understand this strange feeling she was having. She stomped her foot in anger and looked down at her watch. She hadn't dated any boys back home. She had never wanted to. There was no time for that kind of silliness. While other girls were busy painting their nails and learning to put on makeup, she had been training for this year. Her parents had home-schooled her so that there would be more time for combat training. Martial Arts. Weaponry. Self-Defense. She was proud that she excelled in all areas, as were her parents. Socializing wasn't important. Survival was.

She knew she needed to get herself back in control in order to facilitate The Coupling. *Well, if he doesn't put his watch on by tonight, I will fasten it onto his wrist myself while he sleeps!*

She continued looking at her watch, taking deep breaths until the calmness entered her body. Chase didn't understand that coupling with his watch was a good thing, not something to be feared. How could she convey the total feeling of connection and oneness she shared with her watch? She could try to explain it, but she knew he wouldn't truly understand until he experienced it himself. For the first time, she wished she *had* socialized more. Maybe she would have learned the right approach to make him see.

Five days left. If Chase refused to proceed with The Coupling before then, it would all be for nothing. She had two choices. She could convince him to cooperate, or she could force his hand.

Decision made, Alyx set off in the direction of camp to try her hand at apologizing. She would first try to persuade him, and if that didn't work, she would take matters into her own hands.

Just as she took a step in the direction of the clearing, she heard the discharge of a weapon she was all too familiar with. An inferno ray. She took off running, ready for battle.

We've been found!

CHAPTER 12

Chase stared at the destruction in front of him in shock. He blinked twice, looking down at himself to make sure he was still in one piece. When he was positive that no real damage had been done, he whooped and slapped his leg with pure joy.

Alyx burst into the clearing, arm back and ready to release the first blade disc at her target. The scene in front of her baffled her. Her head swiveled back and forth, but she could not find the location of the weapon's shooter.

It took her a full minute to register Chase doubled over with laughter.

"What the..." she yelled.

"Uh...I...didn't...know...that...was...the...trigger..." he chortled. Joyous tears ran down his face, and the more he tried to stop laughing, the more he guffawed.

Alyx slammed her mouth shut, turned around, and stomped back into the forest where she had just emerged only seconds before. *And to think, I was going to apologize to that idiot!*

Her retreating back triggered more boisterous laughter from Chase. Once he started, he couldn't seem to stop.

. . .

Chase inched closer to see what damage had been done to the tree at the far end of the clearing.

"Impressive," he whispered as he walked around what used to be a tree. It was just...gone. A hundred-year-old tree, just gone. All that was left behind was a black, smoking hole. "Wow."

He looked in the direction where Alyx had disappeared and hesitated. He wanted training with these weapons, and she was the only one available. He jogged into the forest, looking for her.

He caught up to her as she paced back and forth muttering to herself.

"Come on, Alyx. I didn't mean to disintegrate a tree, it just, sort of, happened. If you teach me about the weapons, that won't happen again, I promise." Chase smiled his most persuasive smile, flashing his dimples. That smile had been known to melt the hardest of female hearts, and he knew it and used it to his advantage now.

Alyx humphed and continued her pacing. She would stop, look at him, begin talking, and then slam her mouth shut again as she resumed her pacing.

Chase, never one to give up, continued "Please Alyx? I'm a real quick learner, and I'm an excellent shot with my .45, and I'll be more help to you if I know what I'm doing. What was that weapon called, anyway, and where did you get it?"

After a brief hesitation, Alyx blew out a breath. "You are right, but do not touch anything without asking first! You could have blown yourself up, or me for that matter. I need your promise that you will not go shooting things you know nothing about."

"Absolutely. I promise," Chase answered, hand over his heart.

As she walked back toward camp, she began talking. "The weapon you fired is an Inferno Ray. When it reaches its target, it incinerates whatever it hits in less than five seconds. It burns so hot; it causes the object, or person, to implode. That is what happened to your tree."

"Ha-ha! That's awesome! Can I try it again?" Chase laughed.

"No, you cannot try it again! You cannot just go incinerating things. The hunters are looking for us, remember? I will teach you, but we have to remain hidden for five more days. I was actually coming back before to apologize to you."

"Apologize? To me?" Chase blinked.

"Yes. I was out of line when I yelled at you. You are right. It is none of my business who you talk to, as long as you did not tell them anything about me, the watch, or the hunters. Although you are going to have to ditch your cell phone because that is a way for them to track you."

"Get rid of my phone? Aw man, not my phone. Anything but my phone. Let's get rid of the watch instead."

She shot him a look of annoyance, and then visibly calmed herself. They both ducked as they entered the tent together. The tent was built for two, but it was a tight fit, and they were closer than either one was comfortable with. They inched backward as far as they could, backs pushing against the canvas.

Alyx pulled four circular metal discs out of a hidden holster under her shirt.

"These are blade discs. They are similar to your ninja stars. You throw them, and they cut the target in half. I almost released one of these in your direction a few minutes ago."

Chase looked at the harmless looking discs and picked one up. The razor-sharp blade went all the way around the circular disc. It sliced his finger, and he dropped it, sucking at the blood. "Oops. What's this? You used this on the man, right? Back at the house. The hunter?" He held up the weapon she had used the day before in his living room.

"Yes, it is a spark gun. It sends out multiple sparks, which analyze their target in mid-flight. They sense which areas of the body are the weakest, and strike those areas. The body freezes and remains immobile for up to five hours after contact. It can be fatal, but only if a body has a tremendous weakness."

They went over every weapon in the tent; until Chase was satisfied that he at least had some knowledge of each. "Thank you."

"You are welcome. Now choose which one you would like to use to destroy your phone."

Chase winced, then pointed. At least if he had to destroy his phone, he would have fun doing it.

CHAPTER 13

The watch hunters were desperately searching for the two keepers. They were shocked to find out that the girl was here in this dimension out of schedule. She had skipped Dimension 5 altogether, and must have been here in Dimension 6 for two jump times. That kind of anomaly had never happened before, and they were in the dark as to how it was happening now. Never before in the history of dimension travel had anyone been able to thwart the laws of jumping. They had to be stopped before July 7th. Only four days left.

"We need to find them, now!" The woman fumed.

"Yes, and when we do, that girl is mine. I'm still experiencing the after-effects of the weapon she used. She will not appreciate the consequences of shooting me." The man smiled a sinister smile as he thought of what he would do to her when he caught up to her. And catch up to her he would.

They had taken up residence in the boy's house, just in case he was stupid enough to come back home to retrieve something. After a more thorough search of the house, the hunters had still not turned up the watch. They knew the keepers must have taken it with them when they ran.

They had been in the process of tracking the boy's cell phone, but the signal had been lost. They were also in possession of a device that tracked the watches once they were coupled. They hadn't been able to use it to track the watch in this dimension since the boy had not joined with it yet, thereby activating the energy needed for tracking. When the watches were dormant, they couldn't be tracked. Now that the girl was here, that changed things. They could track her. It wasn't an exact science, but it would give them a starting point. But before they left in pursuit of the keepers, they had something else that they must do.

Both hunters were wearing matching necklaces tucked into their shirts. The necklaces were long, with rectangular shaped medallions hanging to their breastbone. The focal point on each was the identical yellow jewel mounted in the middle. They nodded at each other, began counting down "Three, two, one," and simultaneously pushed in on the jewel.

Though the hunters did not possess the watches, and therefore could never travel from one dimension to another, their people had found a way to communicate with hunters in other dimensions, sending them messages through these necklaces. They would alert their people of what, and who was coming in case they failed their mission in this dimension. The girl would not surprise another hunter, at least not in the next dimension. She had lost the element of surprise.

They were sure they were taking unnecessary precautions, but they were meticulous in following their laws. Their Other Selves survival depended on it.

They didn't plan to fail.

CHAPTER 14

He had been as giddy as a child while practicing with the weapons. Alyx could relate to that. As a child, she hadn't played with dolls. She had played with knives. She had even given some of them names. She remembered a boot dagger she had called Daisy after the wildflowers growing in her parent's yard. She hadn't thought it was strange at the time, but looking back now...

Earlier, when she'd tried to broach the subject of The Coupling, he had shrugged it off, saying "I need time to think about it."

We do not have time. Only four more days until the jump, and Chase would need time to adjust once he and the watch became one. She would have to take matters into her own hands, after all. He would thank her for it. Eventually.

She waited until she could hear the sound of his deep, even, breathing, and slowly crawled over to the toolbox where the watch still resided. The lid made a small squeak as the rusty hinges resisted opening, and she reverently took out the watch. She stroked its face and felt the power within. Her watch responded by glowing brighter. The watches were drawn to each other. Just as she and Chase were drawn to each other. Or at least she was drawn to him, she admitted to herself. She thought he was fighting the same attraction she was, but she couldn't be sure.

She crawled to Chase's left side, and very slowly, inched the watch onto his wrist. When she tried to fasten it, the buckle would not hold, and the watch dropped to the ground. He continued to sleep. The hunters could show up to kill them both, and he would likely sleep through the entire scene. She sighed.

Picking up the watch, she tried again with the same results. Suddenly, Chase jerked his arm back. "Hey!"

They stared at each other, eyes glowing in the darkness of the tent, neither one speaking. One minute passed. Then two. Finally, Chase broke the silence.

"I told you I needed time. I can't believe you would do this without my consent. It should be my choice. I should choose my own destiny, not have it mapped out for me. Maybe I don't want to follow someone else's plan. I want to make my own. I know this is what you want, and I guess I believe it's what my ancestors wanted, but I haven't decided if it's what I want."

Alyx had been prepared for anger, but she hadn't been prepared for him to be hurt. Anger, she could relate to. It seemed as if she had been angry since she met him. But she had hurt his feelings, and she didn't know what to do to change that. She hung her head, not meeting his eyes.

"I am sorry. Really. You are right. I am just so frustrated, and we are running out of time. I will give you my promise to let you choose your own path from now on. If it makes you feel any better, the watch would not be forced. After my failed attempt to force The Coupling, I could sense from my own watch that you have to be the one to place the watch on your own wrist. You must accept, and then the oneness will happen. It is your choice, and yours alone, Chase." She placed her hand on his arm.

"Thank you." He reached over to give her hand a squeeze, rolled over, and closed his eyes. He was snoring within minutes.

Men! How can he sleep at a time like this?

CHAPTER 15

Chase woke up with a grumbling stomach. Alyx was sleeping, so he unzipped the tent and climbed out, squinting against the sunrise. He scanned the campsite for food. She must have it somewhere. He walked around the the tent, still searching. *After breakfast, target practice.* If those people came after him again, he was going to be prepared.

His hunt turned up a few granola bars, bottled water, and fresh fruit. "Where is the real breakfast?" He wondered. *This can't possibly be the only food she packed.*

He entered the tent and stopped. This was the first time he had seen her with her guard down, her face completely relaxed in sleep, and he hesitated for a moment, but his stomach grumbled loudly. He didn't feel bad at all as he roughly shook her awake.

"What is wrong? Have they found us?" Alyx jumped onto her feet, and crouched down, ready for battle. He tilted his head. The transformation was fascinating. Even asleep she'd switched into battle mode at lightning speed. *She's kinda cute with her hair all messy and her eyes blinking out the sleep.*

"No, seriously. I'm hungry. Where's the real food?"

Alyx left the tent and motioned toward the granola bars and water. She handed him a banana and turned around, crawling back into her sleeping bag without uttering a word.

"You've got to be kidding! I need real food. Those things out there are snacks, not a meal! Get up. We're going for breakfast."

"I think it would be safer for us to stay here. The fewer people that see us, the less chance there is of coming into contact with the hunters." She mumbled as she rolled over and closed her eyes.

"I don't care what you think. I need food before I do anything else. You can stay here if you want to, but I'm going."

As he strode in the direction of the car, he heard Alyx curse behind him as she ran to catch up. She hopped along on one foot, as she put her shoes on while jogging. Without looking back, he sat down in the driver's seat, started the engine, and smiled. Within seconds she was slamming into the passenger seat, glaring at him. She was obviously not an early riser.

Not sure where they were, Chase drove north. He saw signs for a small town called Apple Blossom fifteen miles away. There had to be somewhere they could eat in Apple Blossom. They drove in silence. He knew enough about girls to know that he had woken her up without giving her any time to prepare herself. She hadn't even gone to the bathroom, which technically was little more than squatting behind a tree anyway, but still. He would wait and let her break the silence. It was better that way.

"I did not even brush my teeth," she growled.

"Um-hmm."

They drove the rest of the way in silence. When they entered the town of Apple Blossom, population 117, he spotted Mervin's Diner right away. He hoped Mervin served big portions because he was hungry enough to eat one of everything on the menu.

As they entered the diner, everyone stopped talking and turned to look in their direction. He held up a hand in a small wave to the room in general. It seemed like half the town's population was currently eating breakfast at Mervin's, and Chase and Alyx were the obvious outsiders. The overly friendly waitress sat them in an orange booth, patched in different places with duct tape many times over in the years since the place had opened its doors. There were varying stages of duct tape, one side appeared to be almost new while the other side peeled back at the edges and had clearly been placed there in a previous era.

Chase ordered a stack of pancakes, an omelet with cheese, toast, home fries, bacon, and sausage. His plate came piled high, and he practically rubbed his hands together in anticipation. He felt as if he hadn't eaten in weeks, and quickly dug in.

Alyx ordered a bowl of cereal and orange juice.

"Ok, so you want me to 'become one with my watch' and all that, and I told you I'd think about. So ... I've been thinking about it. I still have lots of questions that haven't been answered yet. If I'm going to make an informed decision, I'm going to need all the facts first." He paused to shovel more food into his mouth. "It's only fair that I know everything you know, right?"

Alyx met his eyes and slowly nodded in agreement. "I will tell you everything.

But not here. Let's wait until we are alone."

"No problem. After breakfast then. You want a pancake? I can share."

"No thanks, I am full."

Full? How could she possibly be full? Chase signaled the waitress and ordered two pieces of apple pie. "You can't eat in a town called Apple Blossom, and not have a sampling of apple pie."

He ate both pieces.

CHAPTER 16

When they returned to camp, Alyx went to wash off in the creek. She was nervous about the questions that were coming, and she needed a moment alone to compose her thoughts. This may well be the most important conversation of her life, and she didn't want to mess it up. If she wasn't able to persuade him, then she would be jumping to Dimension 7 alone. There would be no choice. It would mean she had failed her entire family line. He had no idea how important this was to her. But he was right. The choice was his to make. She couldn't make it for him; he had to make the decision on his own. She accepted that now.

The hunters now knew who Chase was, and if he stayed here, it was inevitable that they would hunt him down and kill him. Or worse. They might decide to experiment on him. Now that she knew him, she didn't think she could live after jumping and never know if he was alive or dead. But she didn't have a choice. He was so full of life; the thought of him dead didn't compute. Her mind rejected the very notion.

Throughout history, the hunters had coveted the watches. They wanted the power that came along with the watch, but most of all they sought the ability to jump dimensions. They had always hunted the keepers and sometimes managed to take them alive. If that happened, the keeper eventually died, but what they endured between capture and death was unthinkable. The hunters were ruthless in their quest, and they had devised unimaginable ways to torture for many purposes. At first, they had tried to cut the watch off of the keeper so they could wear it themselves. They didn't understand the complete physical and mental connection of keeper with the watch. When that didn't work, they would cut off the keeper's arm, hoping that on the next scheduled jump, just being in possession of a watch would allow them to jump with it. It didn't work that way, but it took the hunters many years to figure that out. When a keeper died, the watch went dormant until the next keeper in that bloodline turned eighteen. Sometimes many years passed between keepers. When the hunters realized it was a blood connection, they became focused on the keeper's blood. They would capture and keep them alive, if you could call it that, just as a supplier of blood so they could experiment with creating their own watches, to no avail. When that also failed, the keeper would eventually be executed. Horrifically.

There had originally been twelve watches total. There are three remaining. All others had been destroyed along with their keepers. Alyx knew that part of her mission was to bring about the extinction of the hunters. There was no other way to ensure that the keepers legacy continued through time. She had succeeded in terminating both hunters in Dimension 4, and she had skipped Dimension 5, arriving in Dimension 6 one month ahead of schedule so that she could meet up with Chase here. It would be her responsibility to hunt and kill the remaining hunters in each dimension she visited. Furthermore, since keepers jumped dimensions in order, and she had skipped a dimension, she had no idea if she would end up in Dimension 5 at all, or if she would go home one month ahead of schedule without ever seeing that place. No one did. So if she never visited 5, it would be Chase's responsibility to continue the war alone in that world. He would have to assassinate the hunters, and she wasn't sure how Chase would react to this knowledge.

She made a decision. She would be completely honest with him, but if he didn't specifically ask her, she would leave out that part of the story for now. She was sure that once he coupled with his watch, Chase would understand.

CHAPTER 17

Chase's eyes landed on Alyx as she emerged from the forest like a fairy, the sun at her back illuminating her outline. He almost expected purple wings to unfurl from her back. She looked like she could be a warrior princess in possession of magical powers. His eyes darted away and he shook his head to clear his brain. *A warrior princess? Where did that come from? I'm getting soft, man.*

His eyes were drawn back to her face like two magnets attracting. He studied her. It appeared as if she had the weight of the world on her shoulders, but would continue to bear the weight. She could handle it. He believed she could handle just about anything. He sauntered over and threw his arm around her shoulder, and lightly punched her in the arm like he would do with Mason. It always made his friend smile, so he was hoping for the same reaction from her.

He noted the surprise on her face, as she looked up at him and a slow smile spread tentatively across her face. She punched him back, of course, though not so lightly. Chase laughed out loud while rubbing his arm.

"Ouch. You sure do pack a punch. You need to learn the difference between real aggression and playful aggression. Try again, lightly this time."

Alyx hauled off and punched his arm harder than the first time. "I am teaching you, remember. I do not need a teacher."

"You could learn some things about dealing with people. You do great with your weapons, but ... Look, I could teach you how to blend in socially, while you teach me Watch Survival 101."

"What are you talking about? I do not need lessons from you. What I need is for you to..."

His face dropped and he blew out a breath. "I know, I know. You need me for coupling purposes. Ok, let's get started then. First question. Why me?"

Sitting down on the blanket, she met his eyes and began.

"I have to start from the beginning, so you will truly understand." She took a deep breath, and continued, "Many years ago, no one really knows an exact year; there was one true dimension jumper. He discovered a way to travel the dimensions and wanted to ensure that the ability would not die with him. His name was Elias Walker. Your ancestor, Chase. Keep in mind that this story has been passed down from generation to generation, so the story may have changed over the years, but the core of it is truth.

He is said to have possessed great scientific knowledge, and a bit of magic, too. No, do not laugh at me, it is true. There are stories of magic throughout history.

Anyway, he forged the very first watch, and connected it with the Gregorian calendar year, which is the calendar we still use today." She paused to take a breath.

"I guess I can be open to the possibility of magic, considering all that I've witnessed in the past few days. So, you're saying my family, the Walker family, began this whole thing?"

"Yes. He chose eleven other men he trusted completely, one from each dimension, and forged eleven more watches, one for each family. Each one created with his own blood. His own DNA. Then they had to wait. Keepers can only be children who are born on the first day of the first month, the second day of the second month, the third day of the third month, and so on consecutively up to the twelfth day of the twelfth month. Only children born on those calendar days have the ability to couple with their family's watch." She paused, and leaned back, placing her arms on the ground before continuing.

"Sometimes many years pass before the next keeper is born, sometimes not. No one knows when a keeper will be born. The watch is activated on the keeper's eighteenth birthday. My birthday is April 4th, and I had a month to complete the coupling before my first jump on May 5th at 5:05. Your birthday is June 6th, and your first jump, if you accept this responsibility, will be on July 7th at 7:07."

"Wait, can you jump to any dimension you choose?"

"No. It is pre-determined. Or at least it has been until now. Until me. Everyone previously has jumped the dimensions in order, beginning and ending with your home dimension. You live in Dimension 6, and your first jump will be 7, followed by 8, 9, 10, 11, 12, 1, 2, 3, 4, 5, finally ending back in your home dimension. My order should have been 5, 6, 7, 8, 9, 10, 11, 12, 1, 2, 3, and returning to 4. My family, the Eris Family, devised a way for me to jump out of schedule. I skipped Dimension 5, so I could jump with you. Never before in the history of jumping has this been done. We don't fully understand what repercussions if any, there will be because of this disruption. Now that we are on the brink of extinction, it was decided that it is worth the risk. Anyway, at the end of your Year of Jumping, you will be presented with one choice. After visiting all dimensions, which one would you like to live in forever? Once you make a choice, it is final. If you choose not to remain in your home dimension, your watch stays in its original dimension, and you jump one last time."

"Did you get any say in this? Who decided it was worth the risk? Your parents? No wonder you didn't want me to choose my path. You were never given the opportunity for another kind of life yourself. Doesn't that make you angry?"

"No. It is my destiny. I've always known, as long as I can remember. I have no regrets."

"Wow, you're a bigger person than I am. I don't like to be told what to do."

She gave a small smile. "I've noticed. There's one more thing you should know before you decide. When Elias Walker forged the watches, he used his own DNA to create them. The watches are powered by your blood, and if you couple with your watch, you will not be able to remove it from your wrist until your year of jumping ends. It will become a part of you. Look closely at the hands of my watch." She held out her arm.

Chase looked down. "What am I looking for?" He continued to stare at it, and when he looked more closely, he noticed there was movement within the blood-red hands of her watch. "Why is it moving?"

"My blood flows through the watch. We are one, this watch and I. As blood is pumped through my body, it is also pumped through the watch. The same will be true of you and your watch. Each watch contains the blood of every ancestor that has worn it. You can commune with your ancestors in a primitive kind of way. You cannot talk to them or anything; it is more like sensing their presence. It is ... wonderful."

"Uh, wonderful? That sounds creepy to me." He continued to stare at the hands of her watch in wonder. "I have one more question for now, please. I have an idea, but I'm not sure I know. Not really. What, exactly, is a dimension anyway?"

"A dimension is a parallel universe. It co-exists with us, but normal people are unaware of its existence. The dimension worlds are the same as ours, but with different outcomes. For example, The North won the American Civil War in your dimension, but in another dimension, maybe the South won. It changes the course of history. If a variation happened far enough back in history, it could alter the dominant species of that world, and nothing will appear even remotely similar to your world. Even the smallest change can have a huge impact."

Chase stood up and ran his hands over his face. This whole thing was unbelievable. He opened his eyes and made eye contact. *So why do I believe everything she said?*

"I think I need some time to think about all of this." He held up his hand when she began to speak. "No, I haven't made a decision yet. This is a lot of information to take in at once. I'm going to take a walk. Alone please."

Looking shyly up at him, she said, "Ok. Chase? Thank you for not laughing at me. It means a lot that you listened. Most people would think I am crazy."

"No problem, it's the least I could do since you came here just for me. I didn't know I was famous in other worlds. Let me know if you want my autograph. Oh, and I do think you're crazy." He winked at her and laughed at her baffled expression as he walked away.

CHAPTER 18

When Chase returned, he scanned the campsite and noticed the change right away. The tent was gone, and there was no sign anyone had been camping here. His eyes moved to Alyx practicing some stretching exercises on a blanket covering the grass. Maybe some kind of yoga? She was so graceful as her body moved; he stood back and observed. Though she appeared totally relaxed as she practiced each move, Chase knew she could segue into full battle mode at a moment's notice.

He thought he was starting to figure her out, especially after hearing a little bit about her childhood. He decided to make it his mission to make her laugh. Not just a small chuckle, he wanted to see a full-on, belly laugh until she cried with joy. She needed to loosen up and learn to have some fun, and he decided he was just the guy to help. Chase thought he would enjoy the challenge.

He admitted to himself that she was getting under his skin, and he didn't know what to do about it. Being from different worlds didn't bode well for a healthy relationship. Best to keep their interactions strictly friendly to avoid future complications. It wouldn't be easy, at least on his end. Sharing the small tent with her had been torture. His body reacted to her in a very non-friendship-like sort of way …

One thing was certain, he didn't want her to leave him here in four days, but he still wasn't sure about the whole watch thing, either. Despite his misgivings, his decision had been made.

After observing her for a few minutes, Chase entered the clearing. He had gone on a run to clear his head and had taken a swim in the river. He felt rejuvenated, and he had come to a decision. He was coming back to tell her what he had decided about the watch. For better or worse.

He could tell she sensed his presence the moment he stepped into the clearing. Her body lost its relaxed pose, and her tranquil expression immediately changed to a questioning look as she made eye contact, silently asking the question she needed answered.

Instead of giving her what she wanted, he asked, "Where's the tent?"

"I have packed everything and put it in the car. We have been here long enough; we need to move to a new location. Soon. We can sleep in the car tonight, and get an early start at dawn." She began folding the blanket as she spoke.

"It seems safe here to me. Why do we need to go somewhere else? I was hoping for some weapons practice, and this is the perfect place for it."

Alyx met his eyes, "The hunters always seem to find us. We think they may be able to track us somehow, similar to how the watches sense the hunters. I'm not taking that chance. We can still get in some target practice while it is light. Maybe you will let me shoot your weapon, too. It's a pretty nice piece. We can have a competition unless you are scared to lose to a girl."

"Ha! Yeah, no problem. I'm not sure I can compete with you, but I'll give it my best shot." Chase smirked as he went to retrieve the gun from the car. He wanted to jump up and down like an excited preschooler. She was in for a surprise. "Ladies first," he said, handing her the weapon.

"How about that tree over there?" She raised the gun, aiming toward a tree at the far end of the clearing, and fired quickly, bark flying as she hit the tree dead center.

"Impressive. Here, let me try." Chase took the weapon, aimed, and immediately fired seven consecutive shots off. Each bullet hit its mark. He began whistling, and walked to the tree, Alyx following closely behind. They stopped to look up at a heart-shape carved by Chase's bullets into the tree trunk. He laughed out loud as Alyx's mouth dropped open.

"Wow, I am impressed. Maybe you are not worthless after all," she said with a smile.

He couldn't contain his joy at simultaneously surprising her and making her grin. *And had she been joking with him?* He hadn't thought she knew how. "Did I mention that I've been shooting a gun since I was eight? Uncle Charlie insisted."

His smile faded, and his enjoyment at the moment waned at the mention of his uncle. "I just can't figure out why he didn't tell me any of this. I didn't think we kept secrets from each other, and this is the secret of all secrets. He obviously knew all about it, and he knew I was about to turn eighteen ... I just don't get it. In his way, he prepared me for this. He made sure I could take care of myself. But he didn't prepare me for this. And now he's dead."

"I wish I could answer your questions, Chase. Maybe he was going to tell you on your birthday. He did not know he was going to die before he had the chance. You will probably never know. You are going to have to learn to accept that there are questions that cannot be answered." She awkwardly patted him on the back. "How did he die?"

"It was a sudden, massive heart attack. It happened so fast. We were eating dinner. One minute he was here, the next he was gone. I called 9-1-1 immediately, but there was nothing they could do to save him. It was exactly one week before my birthday." He looked away for a second to pull himself together. "You know what would make me feel better? Shooting the inferno ray just one more time..."

"You are crazy," she said, but could not deny him after witnessing such vulnerability. Chase watched as she walked to the car to get the inferno ray. "Maybe just once more."

After a satisfying training session, Chase and Alyx settled into the car. She turned toward him imploring with her eyes, and he knew it was time to stop stalling.

"Okay, okay. I've made my decision. I won't torture you anymore. I am going to put the watch on, or 'Couple with it' as you call it, and jump with you to the next dimension on July 7th. On one condition."

"Anything."

"No secrets. I want to know everything you know. No exceptions. We're in this together now, so we do everything together. I can't do this unless I'm completely sure I can trust you."

Alyx hesitated for just a second before saying, "Deal. Let's get started. We do not have much time left," she said as she opened the toolbox containing the watch and reached for it.

Chase held out his hand, "What do I do?"

Just then, Alyx's watch began furiously vibrating, and she gasped. She threw the watch back into the box and slammed the lid while starting the car. "The hunters. They are nearby."

He did not question it. "Are all the weapons packed?"

"Yes, in the back!" She yelled as she fishtailed onto the road at full speed.

Chase crawled into the back seat, roomier than it appeared from the outside, with everything they now owned packed into the back of the Gremlin. "Do you see them?"

"No, I do not ... there!" She pointed with one arm while keeping control of the vehicle with the other.

The hunters had seen them and were in pursuit as they fired their weapons. The amount of space still between the two cars prevented any bullet from finding its mark. The Gremlin was not allowing the other car to catch up. Such surprising power from a small, ugly car. No wonder Uncle Charlie had loved this thing. Chase decided this old car wasn't so bad, after all. He rolled down the window and aimed his .45 back at the black Chevy Malibu. Though he knew his bullets would also fail, he was sending them a message. They would not go down easily.

Alyx headed back in the direction of Apple Blossom. She wanted to stick to familiar roads and try to lose them. Though part of her mission was to take out the hunters, her priority was Chase and his watch. "We have to go someplace safe so you can begin The Coupling."

"I have an idea. I saw an old, abandoned barn near Apple Blossom; maybe we can hide in there with the car. How long will The Coupling take, exactly? And how long will it take them to track us again if we lose them?"

"I do not know. Each keeper reacts differently to The Coupling. You may have no side effects, or it could knock you out for days. We have no way of knowing how your body will react. The hunters already know we are in this area, so they could track us quickly. I just do not know!"

"You work on losing them, ok? We'll figure out the rest."

With each mile, Alyx put more distance between the two cars. They rounded a bend and spotted the old barn. The sun had made the faded red paint appear to have a pinkish tint, and the barn door hung crooked on its broken hinges. Alyx pushed down on the gas. If they could make it into the barn before the Malibu rounded the bend, this might just work.

"Go, go, go." Chase chanted. "I don't see them. Go!"

They flew into the barn, cut the engine, and sat frozen in place.

Within seconds, they heard the sound of the hunter's car speeding by. It had worked. "Yes! High five," Chase laughed and held up his hand. Alyx stared at it, confused. "You put your hand up and hit mine." He reached over and picked up her hand to show her. It means 'Good Job' or 'Way to go.'"

"We cannot stay here. They will be searching this entire area. It's only a matter of time before they find us again."

Chase looked away, then back again. "Let's head back toward home. We lost them, and they won't be expecting us to head back the way we came from. Let them waste their time looking for us here, and I can perform The Coupling at home where I'm comfortable. I have a need to be home one more time since I know I won't be back for at least a year."

"That just might work." Alyx put the car in gear and pulled out of the barn to head back toward Dune Harbor.

CHAPTER 19

They drove in silence, each lost in their own thoughts. Alyx was elated that Chase had finally agreed to The Coupling, but she was beginning to have doubts that they should return home. She was willing to grant Chase any wish he wanted; however, as long as he connected with his watch. She just had to keep him alive long enough to do it.

Eventually, Chase took over the driving, and to her surprise, Alyx fell asleep.

. . .

When she woke, she squinted through blurry eyes at the sign up ahead that proudly announced 'Welcome to Dune Harbor'.

"How long was I asleep?" Alyx yawned.

"A few hours. It sure does feel good to be home." Chase drove straight to the McDonald's drive-through and ordered enough food for five people.

"Why don't you weigh three hundred pounds, the way you eat?"

"It's my metabolism. Wait, if the watch will be powered by my blood, do you think I'll need even more food after I'm joined with it?" Chase chuckled.

"Oh no, we are doomed." She answered on a laugh.

She was becoming more and more comfortable with him. She had been so relieved when he'd agreed to come with her. It was because it was part of her mission, but it was something else, too. She knew she could survive this without him, but she no longer wanted to complete the mission alone. They had worked together in unison during their confrontation with the hunters, and she found that, surprisingly, she trusted him. She liked having someone to bounce ideas off of, and she found that she valued his opinion. She actually ... liked him. She imagined everyone did. He was very charming in his overly confident, almost bragging sort of way. But she now understood that he was not as selfish as he had first appeared.

He laughed and joked to lighten the mood, often to distract her from her own worries. Though at first look he seemed self-centered, he didn't have to try very hard to calm the people around him. It seemed to come naturally to him, and that was a quality she would never possess.

How could so much have changed in such a short period of time? She had planned for many things, but she hadn't been prepared for him.

It is July 5th. Only two more days until the jump.

CHAPTER 20

Chase drove around the block once before parking in the garage. Tension drained out of his body degree by degree when he saw the house still standing in the place it had always been. Part of him had feared that the hunters might have burned the house down, or imploded it, or some other unknown something even more sinister than he could imagine. The house seemed fine by outward appearances. Observing no visible signs of foul play, they cautiously entered through the back door together.

Bodies on high alert, they each carried a loaded weapon at the ready in preparation for a possible surprise attack. As they entered the kitchen, Chase stopped abruptly and scanned the room to take in the destruction. Tables and chairs were overturned, and the refrigerator was lying on its side, orange juice in a slushy half-dried puddle next to it. The rancid smell of sour milk and rotten leftovers filled his nostrils.

He hesitated, then crept into the living room, only to find a similar scene. They did not speak, each sensing that they needed to keep their presence unknown in case somehow the hunters had found a way to find them and had magically managed to beat them here. Anything was possible, he realized now. He thought about the sheltered life he'd led up until now, unaware of all of the mystical things going on all around him. He briefly wished for that ignorance back.

They continued their inspection in each room of the house, ending in the basement. Each room was the same. Evidence of a search, but no current occupants besides the two of them. Lowering the weapons, they relaxed their guard and looked at each other.

"They were obviously still searching for the watch. It feels creepy that they went through all of my stuff. I wonder if they took anything?"

"The only thing they would want is the watch, and we have that. I do not think they would care about anything else. Unless your uncle left something behind that pertains to the watch's history. They would be very interested in something of that nature if it exists. Do you know of anywhere your uncle would have hidden something secretly?"

"Nothing that I know of. As well as I knew him; lately I've felt as if I never really knew him at all. Remember, I didn't know anything about any of this until I met you." He hesitated, a memory nagging at the edge of his brain.

"Unless..." Chase ran up both flights of stairs and entered his uncle Charlie's bedroom, Alyx close on his heels. Just like the rest of the house, the room had been destroyed, and Chase fought a wave of sadness that turned quickly to anger that these people, these hunters, had disrespected his uncle even in death.

He walked past the overturned safe and went to the adjoining bathroom.

"I remember when Uncle Charlie re-finished this bathroom, there was a deep hole where the medicine cabinet hangs. The new mirror did not go as deep as the hole, and I remember he said to me 'Chasey-boy, this would be a good hidey-hole for something secretive if you catch my meaning. Why I could hide my top secret family secrets in here if I had a mind to.' He'd winked at me, and I remember thinking at the time that maybe he was trying to tell me something. There was a mysterious look in his eyes ... but I dismissed it, not realizing we had any family secrets back then, and laughed it off. I didn't think of it again until now." Chase wrapped his fingers around the edge of the mirror and pulled. Nothing happened. "Be right back," he returned to the basement to retrieve a crowbar and ran back, taking two steps at a time, to the master bathroom. "There may not be anything there, but it's worth a shot." He pried at the mirror. After working at it for a few minutes, the mirror gave, first on one side, and then on the other.

Chase shot a quick, surprised look in Alyx's direction, and pulled the medicine cabinet out of the wall.

They both took a step forward to peer into the hole. There, at the far end of the hole, was an ancient-looking wooden box with hinges and a metal latch. It was just a bit smaller in size than a briefcase, only wider. Chase carefully extracted the box, brushing off years of dust and cobwebs. "I didn't really believe we would find anything. I don't know if I want to open it." He sat on the floor with the box in his lap.

"Not open it? Are you crazy? You have to open it! There could be something that would help us in there." Alyx sat in front of him and waited impatiently.

Very gently, as if he feared it might fall apart, he began lifting the lid of the box, and flinched when there was a sudden banging at the door. He slammed the lid shut, eyes shooting up to make eye contact with Alyx. "Should I answer it? I doubt the hunters would knock." He carefully placed the box under the bed and drew his weapon anyway. They couldn't afford to take any chances.

Hugging the wall, they inched down the steps, and slowly peeked out the window. "Oh no, oh no, oh no," Chase said, horrified to see Mason standing on the front porch.

"Chase! Hey, Chase, it's me, Mason. Are you in there? I'm worried about you, man." Mason knocked again and unsuccessfully tried the knob.

Chase whispered to Alyx, "I have to let him in. He won't give up if I don't tell him something. I have to get him away from here. I don't want him involved in any of this."

Though Alyx gave a negative shake of her head, Chase stuck his gun into his waistband and opened the door.

"Hey, Mason! What's up?"

"Why haven't you been answering your phone, I've been calling and texting. You told me your story about being followed and the house break-in, and then you just disappear? I've been going crazy trying to find you, and you say 'What's up'?" Mason pushed past him into the house and froze. "Whoa, what happened here? They came back?"

Alyx stepped out from behind Chase, drawing Mason's attention for the first time. "Hi, I'm Alyx. Alyx Eris," she said, reaching out to pat him on the arm as she had seen Chase do.

"Oh, sorry man. I didn't know you were with someone. Uh, Hi. I'm Mason. You didn't do this, did you?" He gestured toward the ransacked room.

"No. I am helping Chase. We were just getting ready to ... go out on a date, so..."

"Oh. No problem, I'll just get going. Nice watch, by the way. Did Chase tell you about his spooky, mysterious watch, too?" He laughed. Mason could never stay mad for long. "Hey Chase, call me later, ok? We need to talk. But I feel better now that I've seeing your ugly face." He punched Chase in the arm as he spoke.

Chase threw his arm around his best friend's shoulders and punched him back. "At least it's not as ugly as yours."

Chase stood at the door and watched his friend as he walked down the block. He gave one last wave, began to close the door, and the squeal of tires echoed down the street. A black Toyota Camry skidded to a stop near Mason, and a lady with dark black hair jumped out and grabbed his friend. He watched in horror as she injected something into his neck, and threw him into the back seat as his body went limp. She ran around to the driver's side and sped away, all in the span of less than one minute.

Chase sprinted out of the house, but she and his friend were long gone before he was even close. He ran back to the house, "She took Mason. Did you see? She took Mason. What can I do? I don't know what to do?" He paced furiously back and forth. He ran to the garage, got into the car, and took off, in search of some clue. He drove all over town; going up and down each street, but he never encountered a Camry that fit the description. His stomach churned. *How could I let this happen?*

Defeated, he returned home. Alyx was waiting for him. "I am sorry, Chase. She must have stayed here. I assumed both hunters were following us in the Malibu, but it must have been only one of them. He never got close enough for us to see inside the car. And that means the woman has contacted him and told him we are back, so if he is not here already, he is on his way. We cannot stay here. We have to go."

Shoulders slumped, a look of utter hopelessness on his face, Chase nodded. He slowly surveyed the house, realizing that this could be the last time he saw the place. He would be gone for a year at least. He filled a backpack with things he wanted to take with him while jumping, including the wooden box, and went to the car where Alyx was waiting for him. She silently wrapped her arms around him in an embrace meant to comfort. That was all it took for Chase to lose his last thread of control. He reached for her and held on tight. "Mason is the only person left in this world they can use to hurt me. I should have realized that he wasn't safe. Why didn't I think of that? We should never have come back here. It's all my fault. Do you think he's alive?"

"I do not know, Chase. But if he is, I give you my promise we will do everything we can to save him in the two days we have left. You cannot blame yourself. I didn't think of this possibility either. So I guess that means we are equally at fault. If you need to place blame on someone, you will need to include me, too."

He laid his head back against the headrest and squeezed his eyes closed as she backed out of the garage, put the car in gear, and began driving. They had no set destination in mind.

Glancing his way, she whispered, "I think I have an idea where to start our search."

He tipped his head in a slight nod as his mind raced with images of his friend.

CHAPTER 21

Chase couldn't breathe. Bile rose in his throat and he swallowed the bitter taste. *If something happens to Mason, it will be my fault.* He wasn't sure how he would live with himself in that eventuality. Who would talk to Mason's parents if he didn't make it? It would have to be him, but he had no idea what he would say. He was sure they wouldn't believe him if he told them the truth. He would just have to make sure that Mason survived whatever the hunters had planned. If he wasn't dead already... his mind shied away from the very thought. No, he was alive, he decided. He assumed they planned to trade the watch for Mason, and if he were dead, that wouldn't work. He was counting on the hunters keeping him alive until they could arrange some sort of meeting. And if he had to trade the watch for his friend, then that was a small price to pay. He was prepared to trade himself along with the watch if need be. Mason didn't deserve this; he had nothing to do with any of it.

It would also mean giving up Alyx. He was hoping he wouldn't have to choose. Since they would only spend the year of jumping together, he knew that either way they would go their separate ways eventually. He kept those thoughts to himself. Alyx would never agree, but this was Mason they were risking, so there really was no choice.

He had no idea where Alyx was heading, but she seemed to have a destination in mind as she drove as fast as she could while still following traffic laws. It would be end-game for them if they were pulled over by the police and they found the cache of weapons in the back of the Gremlin. They did not have time to waste explaining. If they were to save Mason and initiate The Coupling before the jump time, they needed to make every second count. Chase wasn't sure if he could follow through on his promise to Alyx if the situation with Mason wasn't resolved before that time, but he didn't share those thoughts with Alyx, either.

She parked in the street across from the Happy Home Hotel, though the sign appeared to say ' APPY HO E HO EL' as a result of burned out lights that had never been replaced.

"This is where I tracked them when I was following them before we met up. I don't know if they are still here, but it is a good place to start. If we can find them before they know we are on to them, it will give us the upper hand."

"Let's go," Chase said as he reached for the door handle.

"No!" Alyx reached across him to hold the door shut, preventing him from exiting the car. "We have to make a plan first! If you just walk in there, they will win. We have to be smarter than that. Think, Chase. I know you want to go in there, guns blazing, but that is not going to help your friend."

"You're right. I can't think straight right now. Any ideas?"

"How about a distraction? What if we create some kind of distraction to lure her out of the room? I could distract her, while you go in and get Mason." She began rummaging through the contents of the back seat.

"It could work. What did you have in mind?"

"Just leave the distracting to me. As soon as she runs out of the room, you move, fast. In and out. You get Mason to the car and go. Do not wait for me. Let's agree on a place to meet-up in case we get separated. The Eris Family Motto has always been 'Two plans are better than one,' and for the first time, I think I'm truly beginning to understand it. Any suggestions?"

"How about the marina?"

"That will work. Okay. The marina."

She had loaded up with an assortment of weapons, all small enough to remain hidden. He grabbed his familiar .45, and the spark gun. When she saw him reach for the Inferno Ray, she shook her head, and laid her hand gently on his arm. "The inferno ray is not effective in confined spaces. You would be just as likely to implode the entire hotel with Mason in it. Not to mention it would draw all kinds of unneeded attention. No Inferno Ray. We need a distraction big enough to alarm the hunter, but small enough that we can still get out of here before your police arrive. I think I have just the thing." She exited the car and headed across the street. After a few steps, her watch began vibrating. She looked at Chase. "She is here."

They scanned the parking lot and found the Camry parked at the far end around the corner. They were in luck. No Malibu. Chase crouched around the corner of the building and nodded. Whatever Alyx's plan was, he was ready.

Chase watched as Alyx took a grenade out of her pocket, pulled the pin, and threw it under the car parked nearest to the hunter's hotel room. So much for a small distraction. She ran and hid behind another car. Though the wait only lasted seconds, it seemed like an eternity before the resulting, ear-deafening, *BOOM*. They watched as the woman ran out of the room, cell phone at her ear. Alyx immediately went into action. She charged the woman, throwing her head and shoulders into her gut.

Chase watched in horror. *Can she handle this woman alone?* He couldn't focus on that right now. He had to stick to the plan.

He barged through the still-open door and spotted Mason immediately, lying prone on the bed. Not moving at all. *NO! I'm too late! Mason is dead.*

He crept toward the bed with leaden feet. *Is that ... wait ... did his chest move?* He saw that his friend's chest was, in fact, moving. Just the slightest up and down movement. He was still breathing, though only shallowly. *Yes!* Mason was alive. He grabbed Mason by the shoulders and shook, furiously whispering, "Mason, wake up!" When he got no reponse, he awkwardly picked him up and threw him over his shoulder, one hand holding his friend, the other holding his gun.

The hunter and Alyx were still engaged in a brutal hand-to-hand combat in the parking lot. Hotel guests were standing in their pajamas, watching the scene unfold, snapping pictures but otherwise just gawking. He knew it was only a matter of time before the police would arrive. He turned back to the battle.

There was blood on the hunter's face, and blood on Alyx's arm. Aiming the gun, he lined it up and it only took a split second to realize he had no way of getting off a clean shot. The combination of Mason's weight bearing down on his shoulder as well as aiming at a mobile target made the shot nearly impossible. He could feel the pressure growing in his shoulder and neck as he stood there. It was just as likely that he would hit Alyx, and he wasn't willing to take that chance. *Stick to the plan.* He had to trust that Alyx could hold her own. He'd seen her do it before and he had to get Mason out of here.

He maneuvered Mason into the Gremlin, laying his upper body into the back seat and ran around to the other side to pull him the rest of the way in. With one final glance, he observed as the battle in the hotel parking lot became brutal, and drew in a stuttering breath, blinking in shock. In only a heartbeat's time, Alyx took out a Blade Disc, took aim, and released the blade. One second it was in Alyx's hand, and the next it made contact with the hunter. The blade sliced cleanly through the woman's right arm. She looked down, mouth ajar in a silent scream as she watched her own arm fall with a sickening thump to the ground, a crimson fountain squirting in bursts just below her shoulder that was now only a bloody stump. Using the distraction, Alyx took aim a second time, released another Blade Disc, and the woman's head fell to the ground next to her arm, looking like a horror movie prop. The woman's eyes were still open in horrific fear as the last moment of her life forever froze in place on her now dismembered head, which wobbled away like a cantalope before coming to a face-down stop next to its arm in the street. The headless, armless body, after staying upright for longer than seemed possible, belatedly thumped to the ground to reunite with the other two parts of itself in a macabre reunion, just as the Malibu tore into the parking lot at full speed.

Alyx looked at Chase and yelled, "Go!"

Chase slammed his foot on the gas and took off like a shot. *Stick to the plan. Meet at the marina.* This chant repeatedly continued, over and over in his mind, as he drove in the direction of the marina. He had a new plan once they got there. Alyx would be proud. *Alyx.* She was alone with the man. *She can handle herself.* He had to believe that. *But she's tired from battling the woman ... Don't think, just drive.*

His last thought as he tore through the streets in the direction of the marina was the woman's head rolling on the ground, lifeless eyes staring in his direction.

CHAPTER 22

Chase leaped out of the car the moment he reached Moore's Marina. He knew this place inside and out because Mason's family owned it. He had spent many summers during his youth boating and hanging out here with his friend's family for as long as he could remember. Mason's parents often jokingly referred to Chase as their other son, and he had always reciprocated the feeling times ten. He had been close to his uncle Charlie but had always appreciated having a mother figure in Mrs. Moore, and Mr. Moore was pretty great, too.

He carried Mason out of the car and put him down below in one of the Sundancer cabin cruisers currently docked there, rubbing his sore triceps and lower back from carrying the dead-weight of his friend. He hoped the owner of this boat would not notice it was missing until after he was done with it. He'd briefly considered leaving Mason in the Marina's office but quickly rejected the idea. As long as a hunter was still out there, he wasn't taking the chance of Mason falling into his hands a second time. They would stay together so he could protect his friend.

A slight smile emerged as he read the name painted on the hull of the boat. *Breaking Wind.* He briefly wondered if Alyx would understand the humor. *Alyx. Where are you?* He took one involuntary step in the direction of the car, then stopped, hanging his head. Every molecule in his body wanted to go back for her. *But Mason needs me.*

Chase worked quickly, transporting the entire contents of the Gremlin onto the boat. He found a tarp and threw it over the car. It wasn't the kind of car that would be inconspicuous. There was only one hunter left in this world, but they couldn't relax their guard. He would definitely be out for blood after witnessing the woman's fate, and he worried for Alyx's safety. *What is taking her so long?* Not knowing was torture.

He opened the refrigerator in the office, loading his arms with food and drinks to take aboard the boat, and then filled the gas tank. He sat on the deck and tilted his head, running through a checklist of things they might need, and finally felt confident that he had done all he could to prepare. All that was left to do was wait for Alyx. Mason was still unconscious, and he was concerned about his friend. He had been out cold for some time now, and he had no idea what the woman had injected into him.

He waited. Staring out into the obscure night toward the street, eyes straining through the darkness, he waited. A dozen times, he stood to go for her, then paced and sat back down, running his hands through his hair. And he waited. *Stick to the plan. Meet at the marina.* She would come. She had to. He stood yet again, but this time went below to check on his friend.

He waited what seemed like an eternity, and still, he waited some more. He paced the small interior, then sat, elbows on his knees. Time continued to pass at a crawl, and just as Chase was pushing up to go after her, he heard a faint whisper out of the darkness.

"Chase?"

Rushing above deck, he saw her leaning against the wall of the office. He disembarked and rushed to her side, eyes combing over her injuries. "The man?"

"Still alive. I managed to lose him, but I don't know for how long."

"Can you move?" He asked as he wrapped his arm around her and watched her wince.

"Yes, I think I broke some ribs, that's all. I'll be fine. We have to go. Where's the car?"

"We're not taking the car." Chase pointed in the direction of the Breaking Wind. "Here, put your weight on me." He helped her limp to the boat.

When she was safely on board, Chase started the engine, and slowly backed out, entering the open sea. His movements were automatic. Captaining a boat came as naturally to him as breathing. He hoped the hunter had little or no nautical knowledge. Even if the man managed to find them, they would have the advantage in this setting. He continued to guide the boat into deeper waters, putting as much distance between hunter and keepers as possible.

Alyx was lying on the bed next to Mason, and both looked terrible in their own way. Mason's condition hadn't changed, so Chase took stock of Alyx's injuries. He rummaged through cabinets and located the boat's first aid kit, finding some gauze and slowly wrapped it around her ribs. He was no doctor, but he knew from experience there was nothing that could be done for broken ribs except wrapping them as they healed. He'd broken a rib or two in his football days, so he knew first-hand the pain she was experiencing, but true to her nature, she didn't utter a sound or complain in any way. He was concerned about the cut on her arm, and she had a fat lip that was already scabbed over. As he tended to her wounds, a sudden wave of immense relief overtook him, and he gently took her hand. Looking into her eyes, he whispered, "I couldn't stand leaving you back there, but I find that I trust you completely. I knew you could handle it, but I wanted to be by your side. It killed me to drive away from you. I don't like it when we're apart. I can't explain this feeling; it seems crazy considering we just met days ago. But I feel a strong connection to you. Do you feel it, too?"

Alyx looked away. "You know that I do. We cannot let this distract us from our mission. We have less than a year together, Chase. Let's not forget that."

Chase squeezed her hand, and she squeezed back before dropping his hand and sitting up. "I wish I had thought of food. How will we eat out here in the middle of the ocean? We'll have to go back for food at some point."

"Have no fear, I've taken care of everything. You really didn't think I would forget food, did you?" He winked as he went to retrieve the food stash he had brought onboard.

Though it was mostly of the junk-food variety, it seemed like a feast as they dug in. Apparently, life-threatening situations make a body ravenous. Alyx had never eaten Doritos before, and Chase delighted in the expression of awe that crossed her face as she chewed. He had a moment to wonder what kinds of new discoveries he would make as he traveled the dimensions.

Exhausted, they shared the bed with Mason to try to get some sleep. Though it was a tight fit in such small quarters, they were both asleep within minutes, their last thoughts drifting groggily to the upcoming Coupling as they slept, lulled by the misleadingly gentle rocking of the sea.

CHAPTER 23

Chase woke up and searched the room through squinted eyes. *Where is Alyx?* He checked on Mason, discovering no change in his friend's condition. Brows furrowed, he placed two fingers on his friend's carotid artery and breathed a sigh of relief as he felt the strong pulse beneath his fingertips. Vaguely, he became aware of an unfamiliar sound coming from above-deck. He emerged from the cabin to find Alyx, head hanging over the side of the boat, heaving as she lost the contents of her stomach into the sea.

"Ugh. I'm never eating Doritos again." She moaned as she hung her head over once again. Her violet eyes seemed to glow against the paleness of her face. Each heave aggravated her bruised ribs.

He'd seen many people succumb to the movement of the ocean. It was ironic that such a strong person as Alyx could submit to the sea so easily. "Have you ever been on a boat before?" He asked.

"No." She groaned.

"I think you're sea sick. Let me see if there's anything in the medicine kit to help. Be right back." Going below, he once again rummaged through the kit, finding just what he needed. He returned and handed her a pill. "Take this."

"What is it?"

"It's called Dramamine. It will help, trust me." He handed her a bottle of water.

"Thanks." She stumbled below and collapsed onto the bed next to Mason.

Chase had the morning to himself. He decided to do a little fishing while he waited for Alyx to wake a second time. Or, hopefully, for Mason to wake up, too.

He thought back to his youthful days of fishing with the Moore's, sometimes catching baby sharks and throwing them back into the water. Those were the days. No stress. No deaths. *No watch.*

At the thought of the watch, his eyes were inevitably drawn to his backpack, current home to the watch. It had not been a priority during the events of the past few days, and he had barely given the watch a thought since the man had found their campsite and given pursuit two days ago, though it seemed like a month had passed since that day.

The digital clock on the dashboard read 7:30am Less than twenty-four hours until the jump. He wanted Alyx with him when he began the process, so he would wait just a bit longer.

He could admit to himself that he was nervous about The Coupling, but he would go through with it, nerves or not. There was no way he would be able to live if Alyx left him for good, not after the torture of their short separation last night. He *needed* to be with her. He knew he would go out of his mind if she left him behind. He'd meant what he'd said to her last night; it didn't feel right when they were apart. They belonged together. He briefly considered that the attraction he felt toward her could be the connection of their two watches, but quickly rejected the idea. What he felt for her was real, he was sure of it. No other girl had ever tied him in knots like Alyx did.

There was a sharp tug on his line and his hands wound around and around like a pro. He smiled from ear to ear as he held up the mackerel. "Holy Mackerel! We're eating good today." He chuckled at his own joke.

Fishing was good today. He realized he had missed this simple pleasure. Before he was finished, he reeled in an additional two sea bass and one scup. They would have a sailor's lunch today. He began preparing the fish for cooking.

When Alyx stepped gingerly out of bed, she inched toward the small kitchen, hand on her forehead. Chase was whistling as he fried the fish in a frying pan. Her face, which had started to regain some of its color, went immediately pale again. Chase smiled at her.

"Want lunch?"

"No, thank you. I am never eating again. You went fishing?"

Chase laughed out loud. "I'm a fine fisherman. Argh, matey," he laughed as he flipped the fish over.

"I need some air." She gasped as she went above-deck.

"Did somebody go fishing without me?" Mason stumbled in from the direction of the bedroom, scratching his stomach. "I'm starved."

The spatula flopped to the floor as he grabbed his friend in a bear hug, slapping him on the back. "Mace! Oh, man, you scared me. You've been sleeping for two days. Not getting enough sleep, lately, bro?"

"Uh, Chase...how did I get here, and whose boat is this? The last thing I remember is leaving your house; everything else is a blur until waking up in the cabin just now. What happened? Why don't I remember? And where did you meet the hot girl you were with at your house? Miss Purple hair?"

"Whoa, that's a lot of questions at once, Mace. Let's have lunch, and then I'll explain. So much has been happening...I'm not sure where to begin."

"How about the beginning? Take your time, and don't leave anything out."

CHAPTER 24

"Wait, so you're saying we live in Dimension 6? And your blood will power this watch? And Miss Purple Hair sliced the bad girl into pieces? But there's still a bad guy hot on your trail? That's crazy, Chase. It sounds made up, like a horror movie or something. 'Mwah-ha-ha, the vatch vants to suck your blood.'" Mason pantomimed vampire teeth and neck sucking. "Please, Please, tell me you don't believe all of this. This girl has you brainwashed, man. She's feeding you this line for a reason. It's some sort of con or something. Come home with me. Please, man." Mason drummed his fingers on the table as he spoke, and his leg bounced under the table making the tabletop shake.

Chase took a deep breath. "I do believe it, Mace. Please trust me. It's not just because Alyx told me about it, but also because it just feels right. I don't know how else to explain it to you, but that watch is connected to me. Remember, I told you that day at the beach, and that was before I even knew Alyx existed."

"You know I trust you, man. I do. You have to admit; this story is hard to swallow. If you say it's the truth, then I'll accept that. But if the story you just told me is reality, then I really don't want you to put that watch on, because it means I'll lose you. Why don't we throw the watch into the sea, and let some unsuspecting tuna get zapped into the next dimension? What do you say?"

Chase barked out a laugh, "Great idea ... except it doesn't work that way. The only blood that can power this watch is mine. And it can't be forced; it has to be my choice. Alyx found that out when she tried to put it on me while I was sleeping."

"See? You can't trust her, bro! I told you, you can't trust her. That's proof."

"She apologized, and I forgave her. Water under the bridge and all that. She is a good person, Mason, trust me on this. I can't explain how I feel about her, but I want to stay with her."

"Obviously. You have to fight the power of the hotness. This girl's got you under her spell, but I'll trust you. Not her, you."

Chase rubbed his hands together, "Now let me show you some toys Alyx brought with her from other dimensions. This stuff is awesome, man! You're gonna love it." He took out the bag of weapons and handed it to Mason.

He talked animatedly as he showed each piece to his friend. Mason was almost as excited about them as Chase had been the first time he'd discovered them in the tent. It seemed like weeks ago, but only days had passed.

"And then this tree was just...gone. Just gone, man, you should have seen it. It was amazing. I wish you could have been there."

"Can I try it?" Mason held the inferno ray reverently. "You know my parents never let me near a weapon. I was always jealous that Uncle Charlie taught you to shoot." He shook his head, "I still can't believe he's really gone."

"I know. I keep waiting for him to...just be there." He looked down. "Okay, maybe you can shoot it just once." They emerged from the cabin, running up the stairs like children when the last bell rings.

Alyx was sitting in the Captain's chair. The color was slowly returning to her cheeks, and she seemed in much better shape. "I was just about to come and get you. It's 2:00pm; we only have seventeen hours left before the jump. Chase, we don't have much time. We have to begin The Coupling as soon as possible. I don't know how your body will react, and you have to be prepared for the jump tomorrow morning. Let's get started."

"Uh, yeah, I know, but Mason and I have something we need to do first. Be right back."

He and Mason walked to the stern of the boat, and he showed his friend how to place his hands, fingers spread on either side of the weapon while pushing with all fingers simultaneously. "See, like this. That's how I imploded the tree, I didn't see a trigger, and when I picked it up I must have squeezed in just the right way, and...BOOM."

Mason did as he was instructed, held up the Inferno Ray, aimed at the open ocean, and pushed in with his fingers. *BOOM!*

"Yeah!"

"That's what I'm talking about!"

"Are you kidding? Again? Seriously," muttered Alyx. She nodded her head in Mason's general direction. "He's just as bad as you. Do you have any idea the kind of damage that weapon can inflict? You two are like small children. I cannot believe you. Either of you. Girls would never be this stupid." She stomped below deck, turned around and marched back, grabbed the inferno ray out of Mason's hands, and huffed back down the steps.

Chase and Mason looked at each other for a full thirty seconds of silence, and then they both whooped out a laugh, slapping each other on the back as if they had just won a race. "See? What'd I tell you? It's awesome, right?"

"Yeah, man." Mason beamed from ear to ear. "I wish I could do it again." He looked longingly toward the doorway where Alyx had disappeared. His face fell as he remembered the story Chase had told him. "What will I do without you, bro? I don't want you to go."

"I'll miss you, too. Remember, you'll be starting college soon, and you won't even notice I'm gone. Wait for me on June 6th, next year, after my year of jumping is done. You'll see. It's not forever. It's less than a year."

"If you survive the year."

"Have a little faith in me, bud. I promise you. I'll survive the year. If only to prove your doubts wrong." He smiled.

"I hope you do, Chase. I pray you do." He said, squeezing his friend's arm.

Chase picked up his backpack and carried it down to the cabin. He was ready. Alyx was sitting in the center of the bed doing some kind of yoga pose. "Have you calmed down yet? Because I'm really going to need you for The Coupling. Are you ready?"

She jumped up, "I've been ready for this since before I met you. Are you sure you are ready?"

"As ready as I'm going to be. Let's do this." He grabbed Mason's shoulder and gave it a squeeze. "I've always been lucky to have you for my best friend."

Mason looked directly into Alyx's eyes. "Take care of my guy, here. He better come back after the year is up, or I'll figure out some way to break into your dimension and come after you."

Alyx knew the impossibility of his statement but saw that he was deadly serious. She gave a slight nod of her head before focusing completely on Chase.

CHAPTER 25

It was time.

Chase unzipped the backpack and reached his hand inside to retrieve the watch, and a spark flew when flesh met metal. The familiar electricity immediately charged through the small cabin of the boat, and Chase could feel his body straining toward the watch more than ever before. His blood pumped in time with the clock, and each cell desperately strained toward it. For the first time, he did not try to fight the feeling but instead embraced it, opening both mind and body to the power emanating from the small timepiece. He reached for Alyx's hand with his right hand and squeezed. He looked at Mason, whose mouth hung ajar, and nodded.

He could sense his heart beating and the flow of his own blood as it traveled through his body. Each cell jumped within him like bugs in a jar, trying to escape the confines. Little needles of need poked at his skin.

Likewise, the watch could sense his total acceptance of it and was ready for him. Chase looked into Alyx's eyes as he began fastening the watch onto his wrist. He gasped, looking down as the watch took over, tightening onto his wrist of its own accord. He felt several brief pricks travel all the way around his wrist, similar to a series of medical shots, and the watch truly became one with him at long last as it began drinking hungrily of his blood. There were a few moments of pain, and then...euphoria. Chase smiled a dreamy smile, and welcomed it like a junky taking a hit of his addiction, powerless to resist another moment.

He'd been born for this. Warmth radiated from his left wrist and spread throughout his entire body. He sensed the watch's elation, and it matched his own.

As the watch's hands filled with blood- *his* blood- he watched with wide eyes and mouth slightly ajar. The movement of crimson as it pumped through the hour and minute hands mesmerized Chase, and it was hypnotizing. He didn't know how long he just sat there staring at it, but he could not look away. Nor did he want to.

The boat could sink around him, and still he would not break eye contact, so strong was the connection. It was as if everything he had done up until this point in time had all been leading to this very moment, right here and now. He was in a euphoric state of mind, body, and soul. At that moment, he was alone in the cabin with the watch, everything and everyone else faded into the background as he and the watch became one in every way.

Before his eyes, the watch began a magical and massive transformation. All at once, the watch's band shifted from the familiar old worn out leather, to what appeared to be some kind of alien metal. The closest comparison Chase could make was to that of a bronze metal, but he quickly rejected the comparison since even that didn't accurately describe the substance. He was at a loss for the right descriptive words because nothing in his experience truly compared. It seemed to shimmer and move from within as though not a solid at all, but instead some kind of liquid form contained inside the solid outer form. Though when he reached out and touched the band, it felt solid to his touch.

The watch face shifted from a circle shape to a rectangular shape, and the old, scratched glass covering the face seemed to melt away as a new substance formed, becoming solid while they sat observing. It was similar to glass in its translucence, but he sensed it was much stronger. He need not fear that this material would shatter on impact. This watch, he instictively knew, was virtually indestructible.

The rectangular shape shifted yet again forming a blocky hexagonal shape. Within the face, there appeared a horizontal thick cobalt line from number nine to number three, and a thinner intersecting vertical cobalt line connecting numbers twelve and six. For the first time, Chase noticed that the numbers on the face of the watch were also filled with his blood. The number 6 was slightly larger than the other numbers, obviously marking his home dimension. Lastly, a thin iridescent, midnight blue color traveled around the entire outer edge of the watch, and as he looked on, it began to gently glow the same dark blue color. And then just as quickly as it had begun, the watch went still.

Chase continued to stare at the watch. He could not tear his eyes away. The previously mysterious Coupling was not, in fact, something to be feared after all. He finally understood how Alyx felt about her watch. They were One. He reached out and tentatively stroked the face of the watch, just before he collapsed onto the bed, unconscious.

CHAPTER 26

Alyx blinked away tears of joy as she witnessed The Coupling. She remembered, just two months previously, experiencing the same feelings of joy when she and her own watch had become one. No normal person could ever understand what it meant to be a keeper. It was a miraculous merger of keeper to watch, as well as a huge responsibility.

The watches had the ability to look deep into the current keeper's mind and body, and transform in appearance to match each wearer's personality. Her own watch had chosen purple to represent her, and Chase's had chosen deep blue to represent him. It was...perfect.

She felt proud of Chase and delighted for him. She admired his ability to adapt to every situation, despite being in the dark his entire life. She herself had always known about her destiny as a keeper of the watch, but Chase had made the decision in such a short period of time and without much information. He trusted so easily, and she was humbled that he had offered her his complete trust in just a week's time.

At the same time, she had mixed emotions about spending the better part of a year by his side. She was already growing attached to him, and she wondered how she would ever leave him at the end of their jump time. And when he smiled at her, his dimples showed, and heart heart tripped ... Alyx pushed that thought aside and focused on the magic currently going on in the cabin of this small vessel. They had to resist this attraction they had for each other. It couldn't interfere with the mission. She didn't want to miss any part of Chase's Coupling due to daydreaming; she wanted to be as much a part of this moment as she possibly could. Just then, Chase collapsed backward onto the bed, and Mason ran to his side.

"What happened, is something wrong?"

"Nothing's wrong. Each keeper's body reacts differently to The Coupling, and I knew this was a possibility. He'll be fine." She looked at the clock. It was 5:53.

Approximately thirteen hours until the jump. She wondered if there would be a problem jumping if Chase was still unconscious. She had no way of knowing. She herself had coupled weeks before her own first jump, so she couldn't compare her situation to this one. Throughout history, as far as she knew, keepers initiated The Coupling long before their jump time was scheduled. She had never heard tales of a keeper making the jump *while* Coupling.

Just then, the cabin heaved violently back and forth. She and Mason raced out of the cabin to be greeted by a wall of blackness, blown backward by a strong gust. A storm was blowing in, and Alyx for once had no idea what to do. She turned troubled eyes to Mason. "Tell me what to do."

"Oh, man, this is bad. There's nothing we can do right now except ride out the storm, and hope when it passes we're still afloat. We are at the mercy of the sea. Get below!" Mason waited for Alyx to precede him, and then followed her into the cabin. They ran below and closed the door. The tiny cabin offered little protection against an onslaught of this magnitude, and the small boat rocked precariously back and forth against its will. Alyx's face went immediately pale, and she clutched her stomach seconds before she stumbled into the tiny bathroom.

The storm raged on for what seemed like hours, and Alyx was sick the entire time. She couldn't remember ever in her eighteen years of life feeling sick like this. *Is this what it feels like to die?* She wondered. She thought that was a distinct possibility. Finally, she lay down on the bed next to Chase and fell into an exhausted slumber.

CHAPTER 27

Mason huddled alone in the corner of the cabin, hands shaking. Eyes darting to the bed, he wished for the hundredth time that Chase would wake up so he would know for sure that his friend was okay. This whole thing was crazy. If he hadn't witnessed it with his own eyes, he never would have believed it was possible. Chase trusted Alyx, but Mason did not share his optimism. He still thought it was possible that his friend had fallen prey to some kind of a con. Mason knew Chase always found the good in people, sometimes at his own expense. Admittedly, he had witnessed the watch's magic, but he wished his friend had chosen to get rid of the watch and stay here. He hadn't been joking when he had suggested throwing the thing into the ocean. Now that the watch had connected with Chase, there was no going back. He was concerned about these so-called other dimensions, and he feared for his friend's safety. His imagination ran wild as he thought about all the things Chase might encounter on his inter-dimensional travels.

The storm was one of the most brutal ones he could remember. Mason felt at times as though they were a toy ship in a bottle, heartily shaken by a toddler as the ship and passengers bounced off the glass walls inside. As he looked on, water poured down the steps and under the door, soaking the floor of the cabin. The small craft rocked and moaned. If this storm didn't subside soon, he was going to get seasick, too. Or the boat was going to sink to the ocean floor. Neither option sounded appealing.

Sitting on the wet floor with his legs bent, Mason laid his head on his knees and recalled summers spent boating with Chase, fishing and just hanging out. Chase had always been the better fisherman. Fish were always biting when his friend dropped his line. He remembered days at the beach surfing or tossing a football, and later as teenaged boys on the beach girl watching. They didn't agree on girls. Chase preferred dark-haired girls with long legs, while Mason preferred short blonds and freckles. No matter the type, all the girls seemed to gravitate toward Chase with his suntanned good looks, but Mason had never been jealous. He understood. People were just drawn to Chase. Just as he had been when they first met as kids. Chase had spent a lot of time playing sports and working out, while Mason had been more interested in playing video games. But somehow their friendship seemed to work.

Mason wasn't sure how he would survive the next year if he couldn't even send Chase a text. He had known they wouldn't see as much of each other while he was at college, but at least they would have been able to stay in communication with each other. When Chase left, they would be completely cut off from each other. He wouldn't know if his friend was alive or dead. He shied away from the thought as soon as he had it. As he sat huddled on the floor hugging his knees, he almost wished he could go along with Chase on this yearlong adventure. Almost. A shiver traveled the length of his body.

The clock read 8:02pm Though the boat had been tossed around for hours, he could sense the storm was losing momentum but not over yet. If Alyx's story was true, that meant there were only eleven hours left until the infamous 'jump' he kept hearing about. Eleven hours left with his best friend, who was currently unconscious. Leave it to Chase to miss their goodbye. He walked over to the bed and shook his friend. "Hey, wake up." Alyx's eye cracked to stare up at him uncomprehendingly, before fluttering closed once again. Chase gave no response. Mason felt for a pulse, and after finding a strong heartbeat, relaxed just a bit. He reached toward the watch and stroked his finger over it, pulling back when he sensed an unnerving awareness from within. *Creepy.*

He went above deck to survey the storm and his shoulders relaxed a bit when he gazed over the horizon. Through the quickly darkening dusk sky, he could see the rain had just about stopped. In the far distance, he spotted blue skies behind the gray. When he looked toward the bow, the sky appeared stormy and dark, but when he turned toward the stern, as the sun set it looked like another world with its opposing clear skies and white clouds. Almost like another dimension, he chuckled silently to himself. He briefly wondered what it would be like in one of the other dimensions. Mason decided he was relieved that he was not the one born into this responsibility. He began cleaning up the debris left over from the storm and then sat down to think. He must have dozed off because he was awoken suddenly to the sound of a helicopter hovering in the distance. The wind was still unpredictable, and the pilot seemed to be having difficulty controlling the huge metal bird. Why would anyone fly in this kind of weather? Mason wondered.

Maybe the pilot needed help. He ran back into the cabin, and past the two sleeping figures, retrieving the binoculars he had seen there.

"Hey, Sleeping Beauties, anyone awake? No? It figures I have to do everything myself..." Mason mumbled on his way past the bed.

Returning above, he aimed the binoculars in the direction of the helicopter, just as the pilot looked back at him through his own set of binoculars. The man looked a bit familiar... but he couldn't place him. He couldn't make out the man's facial features behind the spyglass, but he was able to glimpse the midnight black hair above the binoculars. He couldn't recall where he had seen hair like that before...it seemed vaguely familiar, but he just wasn't sure. Mason waved and tried to radio the 'copter with no success. He ran below again, trying once more to wake his two sleeping crewmates. Chase did not move, but Alyx opened one eye a slit.

"There's a helicopter. I think it's in trouble." Mason bounded out of the cabin.

Alyx managed to drag herself above deck. Shielding her eyes from the light, she looked upward and gasped.

"The hunter! He's here to kill us." She immediately went into action, running below to retrieve her bag of weapons and then raced back. In her weakened state, she wobbled on her feet, and at the next big wave, she fell and hit her head on the port side of the boat. "The weapons," she moaned, "Use the weapons." As she reached up to put her hand on her head, it came away covered in blood.

The helicopter was fighting the wind as it closed the distance between itself and the boat.

"Hey, maybe that's just an innocent bystander." Mason once again raised his binoculars, just in time to witness the man aiming his gun toward their small boat. This was no innocent.

"He's shooting at us. Find cover!" Bullets bounced off the Breaking Wind's hull.

Mason rummaged through the bag and quickly grabbed the first weapon he put his hands on. The Inferno Ray. He tried to remember everything Chase had said about firing this weapon. In his panicked state, he worried that he would do something wrong. He wasn't comfortable around weapons like his friend was. What if he aimed the wrong direction and blew up the boat?

"Be careful. You need to have control of it to be accurate," Alyx instructed.

He raised the weapon, only to fall backward as the boat was tossed by another strong wave. The inferno ray skidded across the deck. As he crawled after it, he felt bullets whiz past his head and saw holes appear as they made contact with the hull. He retrieved the weapon, wedged his feet between the seat supports, and stood up. His arms felt like jelly as he held on to the alien gun. He could do this. He had to. This guy was trying to kill them.

Putting his fingers in the proper placement on either side of the weapon, he pushed in with all his might. The weapon fired toward its target...and missed. He ducked as the man in the helicopter continued firing toward him. *Breathe.* Mason took a deep breath. "Do I need to reload this thing or something?" he yelled over the wind.

"No, it recharges itself. It just takes a minute," Alyx called back. "I'll cover you."

She grabbed another unfamiliar weapon out of her bag and aimed. Blood dripped from her forehead, and Mason thought she looked fiercer than any warrior as she fired. The resulting explosion took out one of the helicopter's blades, and the chopper began a downward spiral heading straight toward them.

"Now!" Yelled Alyx, as Mason set his stance and aimed once again. With the helicopter spiraling, he feared that he would miss yet again. He only had one chance to get this right. All of their fates lay in his hands. He blinked and remembered that he was an expert Gamer, and thought of all the times he had theoretically saved the planet in cyberspace. Once again, he placed his fingers in the proper placement, put on his game face, and pushed in.

The Resulting *BOOM* rocked the boat precariously side to side. Mason and Alyx held on with all their might, eyes glued to the spot where the 'copter had been. The helicopter and pilot were gone. Just gone. One minute they were there, and the next...gone. Poof. Vanished. It was as if a vacuum had sucked everything toward the center until it disappeared. All that was left were great wisps of black smoke spiraling in the air, and the burning smell of fumes.

Mason stood, just staring at the empty space. His body began shaking, little tremors that started in his arms and traveled through his body. His teeth chattered. He didn't know how long he stood there. When he came out of his trance, he became aware of a hand on his arm.

"You saved us."

He looked at Alyx, at first not able to comprehend her words.

"I-I killed that man. Those are words I n-never thought I'd say. I don't know how to feel about that." Mason couldn't make his body move. The tremors shook his body again, uncontrollably. His legs gave out and he sank to the deck.

"You had to. You saved us. All of us. Me. You. Chase. If you hadn't fired, we would all be dead. Thank you." Alyx squeezed his arm.

"Y-You're right. I-I know it. But it still doesn't seem right. S-So, that was a hunter, huh? N-Not so tough if you ask me."

"Hey guys, what did I miss? What's that smell?" Chase emerged onto the deck greeted by the now-clear, but steadily darkening skies of the dusky evening.

CHAPTER 28

"You what?" Chase stared, eyes wide, brows raised. *Mason* had taken out the hunter? The same Mason who wouldn't even squash a bug? The same guy who threw back all the fish he caught just to avoid killing them. His friend had the softest heart around. He just couldn't wrap his brain around the idea.

"Way to go, Mace. I wish I could have seen it! I always knew you had the heart of a soldier," Chase laughed. When his arm reached out to slap Mason on the back, he glimpsed his watch. It lightly glowed the same deep blue color as before. He paused. It made him feel connected. As though he wasn't alone in the vast, dark world. Though he was immensely relieved it had transformed its appearance so completely. Now, it was... cool. He would have hated to wear it as it had looked before The Coupling, all old and ancient-looking.

He looked at Alyx, "Let's take care of that cut." He retrieved the first aid kit and took out some gauze. As he was cleaning her wound, he began talking. "Ok, so now what?"

"Now, we wait until 7:07 tomorrow morning, and then we go."

"Can we take anything with us? Or will we arrive...naked?" He wiggled his eyebrows, his eyes traveling the length of her body.

With pink cheeks, she snapped, "No! We will still be dressed! Anything on your body will jump with you. If you have your backpack on, it will come. That's how I brought the weapons from other dimensions along when I jumped here."

"Where will we...uh...land?" Chase asked.

She frowned. "It's not an exact science, but I've been thinking about that. Though you don't jump to the exact spot, you usually end up somewhere in the vicinity of the location you left from. Though you may not recognize anything you see when you arrive..." her eyes clouded over for just a split second. "But I've been thinking; if we jump from here, it's possible we could end up in the middle of the ocean without a boat. I think it would be best for us to find land and leave from there. How long will it take to make it back to the dock?"

"A few hours. We can make it. We still have, what, like ten hours before we go, right? If we turn around now, we'll have no problem." He made eye contact with Mason, who took the wheel and in minutes they were headed in the direction of the shoreline. Toward home. It seemed somehow fitting that he should jump from the only place he had ever known as his home. He wouldn't want it any other way.

"So, while I was sleeping, I was kind of talking to my ancestors. I guess talking isn't the right word, exactly. Not with words or anything, more of a feeling. Each ancestor has a different feeling, I guess. Oh, man, I'm messing this up, but I don't know how to explain it another way." Chase shook his head. "Did that happen for you?"

"Yes. I once told you it is amazing, remember? I do know what you mean, Chase." Alyx squeezed his hand.

"Ugg! You two are psycho." Mason hummed the music from the 'Twilight Zone.' They both ignored him.

Chase looked at Mason, "I dreamed, I guess it was a dream, that Uncle Charlie was talking to me. I know this sounds crazy, and I don't even know if it was anything other than a dream, but..."

Both sets of eyes locked on his. "He said he was proud of me. And that he was sorry. He'd wanted to tell me about...all of this...on my birthday. He said he wanted me to have a normal life, and that he didn't want me to be burdened with this unless I chose to be. He would have told me on my eighteenth birthday and given me a choice. If he had lived. Dream-Charlie said he was proud to raise me after my Dad left. I never knew my parents, I've been with Charlie for as long as I can remember," he looked at Alyx as he spoke the last. "My father left me with my Grandfather and Uncle Charlie and never came back. I don't know much about my mother, except that she was going to give me up for adoption, but Granddad and Charlie took me in. With all I know now, I have to wonder what really did happen... I may never know. Maybe he didn't leave me, after all. Maybe the hunters got to him because of my family's heritage. Maybe they were trying to find the watch. I don't know."

"Chase, when was your Dad's birthday?" Alyx wondered.

"I have no idea, but Uncle Charlie's birthday was February 2nd."

"No wonder you can feel your uncle so strongly. He was a keeper! That makes sense. He wasn't just guarding the watch for the next keeper. He was one himself. I don't believe it was a dream, Chase. I think your uncle found a way to communicate with you."

Chase gave an affirmative nod. "Yes, that's why I can feel him so strongly now. It's like I still have a part of him with me. Well, for this year anyway. It's nice. The thing is, as crazy as it sounds; I think I can feel my father, too. The connection is much vaguer but...is it possible two brothers from the same family were both chosen as keepers?"

Alyx considered for a moment. "Anything is possible, Chase, but I don't know the answer. Sometimes many years pass, and a generation is skipped, but I'm not sure if it's possible for both siblings in the same family to be chosen."

"Ok. At least I have Charlie with me." He indicated the watch. "So, what will we do for a whole month in Dimension 7? Other than avoid the hunters and try to stay alive?"

Alyx hesitated for a brief moment before answering. "We will observe each dimension's advancements and take notes to be compared with all the previous keeper's recorded historical notes. We will stay alive and guard our watches to prevent their extinction. We will protect the secret of the keepers, as Elias Walker commanded. And we will try to discover the location of the keeper of the third watch, the last remaining watch, and if we succeed, protect that keeper and watch as fiercely as we protect our own. We do not even know if he, or she, has been born yet." She refused to make eye contact, got up and walked to the bow of the boat, staring out over the now black sea.

"Is something wrong?" Chase went to stand with her.

"No, everything is happening exactly as it should."

It was 10:30pm Nine hours and thirty-seven minutes until the jump.

CHAPTER 29

"Is there any food left on this boat? I'm famished." Chase searched through the kitchen, digging up a bag of chips, two granola bars, and some candy bars left from the stash he had brought onboard. "I need to eat. We're gonna need more food."

"Is food all that you think about?" Alyx smiled.

"Hey Mace, you want me to take over?"

Mason shook his head, "I got this. You should probably rest before morning. "

"Rest? I've rested enough. I feel an excess of energy right now. I feel...powerful, like I could single-handedly take on an army of hunters. It must be the watch. I don't know." Chase flexed his muscles as he spoke. "Do you think we'll have time to stop for breakfast before the jump? After all, we don't know the food situation in the next dimension, so..."

Mason laughed, "It's always food with you, man. You should be the one that needs to lose weight, the way you eat. Where does it all go?" He shook his head.

"How far are we from shore?" Chase wanted to know.

"About an hour out, it won't be much longer. I've been thinking. How will I explain the condition of this boat, which we don't own by the way, to my parents? I'm in deep trouble if they find out I had anything to do with this. What if the owners have reported it missing? That involves the police, and I can't have a record. That would effect college, especially since I'm going for Criminology. You're going to be gone, and it'll just be me left to explain."

"You're right; I'm sorry to leave you with this mess, man. We should be early enough to dock before your parents open the marina. Let's clean up as much as we can, and then the only mystery will be the bullet holes. Not much we can do about that. The owner's insurance should cover it." He began straightening up in the cabin. "If we put the boat back, hopefully it will be a few days before the owners feel like sailing. No one would have any reason to suspect you had anything to do with it when they discover the damage. All you have to do is play dumb."

"You know I'm a terrible liar, Chase. My parents will know I'm guilty if they look at my face."

"Well, then tell them the truth, and they'll lock you up in a mental hospital. Your choice." Chase winked, as Mason punched his arm.

In the thick darkness of night, they approached the marina. Mason throttled back for a quiet, stealthy approach. Chase scanned the dock. The marina seemed deserted, as it should be at 4:10am

"What do you want to do with our last three hours, Mace? After eating, of course. It's your call, man."

"'Annihilation,' dude. Let's play one final round of 'Annihilation.'"

"You're on!" They whooped like children as they fist-bumped.

Alyx, a look of confusion on her face, wanted to know, "What is 'Annihilation'?"

"Aw man, you mean you don't have 'Annihilation' in your dimension? You're missing out!"

"It's only the most popular online video game on the planet."

Her mouth fell open in disbelief. "Men. I do not understand how you can waste your time playing video games at a time like this! We only have a few hours left, and you are talking about playing a game?"

"What else do we have to do? My bag is packed. Your bag is packed. The hunters are dead. I'm ready. Now my priority is spending time with my best friend before I go away for the better part of a year. That's the most important thing I can do in my last hours."

"I'm sorry, you are right. You should spend time with Mason. Okay, maybe you two can show me how this game works." Alyx rolled her eyes as she spoke.

They docked the Breaking Wind, uncovered the Gremlin, and drove toward Chase's favorite diner for an early breakfast. He was beginning to see why his uncle had loved this old car so much. He was starting to think maybe it was a classic, after all.

CHAPTER 30

After breakfast they drove back to Chase's house in silence, each lost in their own thoughts. As Mason called his parents to let them know he had spent the night at Chase's, Chase set about cleaning up some of the mess left behind by the hunters, and then settled in to play his farewell game of 'Annihilation.' Gaming was the one thing Mason excelled in, so Chase knew he was about to be bested by the best, but he was okay with that. This is what he and Mason did; they hung out.

Chase glanced at Alyx. She wasn't at all interested in the game. She had a look of sheer concentration as she loaded, and then re-loaded her bag, making sure everything was ready for the jump. He thought he even heard her talking to herself periodically. He was a bit nervous about it, but he was ready. His eyes cut down to his own bag on the floor. He looked at his watch. 6:00am Only one hour and seven minutes left.

"Aw man! You're dead. Are you paying attention?" Mason was very serious when it came to gaming.

"Yeah okay, okay. Sorry. Go again." For the next hour, Chase focused all his attention on the game.

"Chase," Alyx said. "Time to go, Chase."

"Huh?"

"We have seven minutes until the jump. It is time to go."

Chase and Mason blinked in unison, as if coming out of a trance, and looked at Alyx. Chase nodded his head and put down his controller. He looked at Mason.

"I guess this is it, man. Will you take care of the house while I'm gone? I'd like to know I won't be living down on Gull Street under the bridge with the homeless community when I get back. That wouldn't be a very happy birthday present if you know what I mean."

"Yeah, sure. No problem. It'll give me a place to crash when I'm home on break. I'll tell my parents your uncle left you money or something, and you're taking a year off to travel the world. It's mostly true, although you'll be traveling different worlds, but they don't need to know that part. " Mason gave Chase a huge bear hug. "I'm really gonna miss you, man."

"Me too. Thanks for everything, Mace. I mean that. I'm sorry I got you involved in this." Chase took a step back and looked at Alyx. "Now what?"

"We wait. We don't have to do anything; the watch does all the work. Do you have your bag on you?"

Chase indicated the bag on his back. 7:06am One minute to go.

Alyx looked deep into Chase's eyes, and said "Uh, Chase. There is something I did not tell you." She took a deep breath, and continued, "This is going to hurt. Bad. See you on the other side." Chase didn't have time to respond.

7:07.

Electricity immediately filled the room, as the static electric hum charged through each of their bodies. He saw Mason step back just as the watch tightened on his arm bringing on a small flash of pain. *That's what she calls pain? No sweat,* Chase thought. The watch began glowing so brightly, he had to look away.

Both watches together illuminated the entire room as purple and cobalt combined. He saw the blue move slowly through his veins as it traveled up his arm moving away from its origin as if the blood itself had turned an iridescent sapphire. Fascinated, and slightly horrified, his eyes tracked the cobalt flow up through his veins, his neck, and into his face. Looking up, he saw that purple also illuminated throughout Alyx's veins making her look surreal, and realized he must look the same to her.

Two separate translucent and ever-changing pools appeared above each of their heads, giving the illusion that the ceiling above them had disappeared. The substance had the silvery shine of mercury in a thermometer, and it seemed to float above them, as if alive. The dual pools began to lower toward them, slowly at first. He looked up in awe and disbelief and briefly considered running. Briefly. He knew it was too late to turn back now. All at once, the silver pool lowered itself completely in one swift movement, consuming him all at once.

And then the real pain began.

CHAPTER 31

It was a pain like nothing he had ever experienced. Chase's life up until this moment had not given him the knowledge that agony like this even existed. His body felt as if tiny claws were pulling it in every direction simultaneously, and yet he burned from the inside out. Though unbearable, he managed to form only one thought. Just one.

Alyx.

He was dying. He was sure of it. And Alyx would be alone. That was the last coherent thought he managed before the excruciating pain made thinking nearly impossible.

Another wave of tortuous energy surged through his body, and he struggled to form another intelligible thought in his fried brain. He waited for his body to combust spontaneously, and wished it would happen quickly. It was the kind of pain that makes you hope for the end. Wave after wave racked his body for what seemed like an eternity, but in reality, it lasted only one full minute. Just as suddenly as the pain had begun, it ceased. His tormented body did not at first compute that it was over.

Chase lay prone in fear of triggering another nightmarish wave. As reality came slowly back to him, he realized he was lying on his back, his body stiff as a board. He experimentally moved one finger, and when no pain followed, he moved his whole hand. He realized he was still lying stiffly on his back, with arms outstretched on either side of his body, and legs apart in a star formation.

He soon became aware of a familiar, soothing, sound. Though his brain acknowledged that it was familiar, he couldn't seem to put the last piece of the puzzle into place to deduce its origin. Chase realized his eyes were squeezed tightly shut, and he made a halfhearted attempt to open them. Gingerly, he opened one eye just a slit, only to slam it closed again because of the scorching brightness.

His body felt weightless as if it was floating and, since the pain had disappeared, he was content to stay in this transitional state forever. He wondered if he had died and was now hovering in Heaven awaiting his entrance through the Pearly Gates, and he welcomed his fate. If it was his time to meet his Maker, he would accept that.

Time passed, and Chase continued to lay inert. The soothingly familiar sound remained a focal point in his slumberous state. He slowly rolled onto his side and curled into the fetal position. He would be content to remain in this state for eternity, if it meant the pain was truly gone. When the movement of his body did not trigger a new wave of pain, Chase started to become more aware of the sounds around him.

The repetitive sound of white noise was interrupted by the occasional ... squawking sound? He knew that sound ... *A seagull! The beach!* Chase forced his eyes open against their will and realized he was lying in the sand, the soothing sound now clearly identified as the ebb and flow of ocean waves. His eyes watered from the brightness, but he raised his arm to shield them as he squinted through the light.

Sluggishly, he forced his unwilling body into a sitting position and surveyed the scene around him. His breath came in short gasps. The beach was deserted. He inhaled a sigh of relief that there would be no witnesses to his current condition. His body was as weak as a newborn baby's. He focused all his energy on his breathing, and all at once reality came into focus.

Alyx! Where is Alyx?

"Alyx!" He rasped. Turning his head, he couldn't see her anywhere on the empty beach, or find evidence in the sand that she had been here with him at all.

"Alyx!" Chase unsteadily got to his feet and took a few wobbly steps. He became aware of the weight of the backpack on his back, and the cold water seeping through his sneakers.

Where is she?

He remembered they had been standing next to each other when they had jumped. *Ha!* 'Jumped' was not an accurate description of what he had just experienced. More like consumed. As if his body had been consumed from the inside out by an acid-like substance. Whoever had named the transfer of a body to another dimension a 'jump' had been deranged. They should have given it a more accurate name, like 'The Consumption,' or another more frighteningly descriptive adjective.

"Alyx!" With each step, Chase's body regained its control a bit more, and he could feel the energy returning to his depleted muscles. He squatted to splash cold seawater on his face and let his eyes roam the beach around him. *Where could she be?* He wasn't sure which direction to go, or where to begin his search.

Had there been a problem with her jump? Her family had altered the order in which she traveled the dimensions. Had they messed with something they didn't truly understand, and now Alyx was paying the consequences? He had seen her swallowed by her own silvery substance just as he had been, so he knew she had most likely traveled... somewhere. Could she have jumped backward, since she had skipped Dimension 5 to get to him in Dimension 6? Or because they had defied the laws of jumping, had she jumped back to her home dimension, prematurely ending her year of jumping? Maybe two keepers had never jumped dimensions together before because it was an impossibility. Chase shied away from another, more sinister possibility. He would not allow himself to believe that she had come to harm in some way.

He paced a frantic path in the sand, unsure of what to do next. Where would she go if she were here? An answer immediately came to him.

The house.

Chase decided on his plan of action and set off. If he were indeed in Dune Harbor, he would go to the house and wait for her. He was sure she would do the same, and they would meet up there.

Decision made, Chase began walking.

CHAPTER 32

With each step, his limbs regained more energy. When he cleared the dunes, he looked around to get his bearings. He was familiar with every beach in Dune Harbor, but he did not recognize the street he was currently standing on. He continued walking and glanced down at his softly glowing watch. It peacefully glowed 7:45am

Where are all the tourists? On a normal July morning, vacationers could be seen renting bikes, searching for seashells, or jogging on the sand, but as far as the eye could see, no one was around. Looking at the watch once again, he voiced, "Ok, Charlie, which direction should we take?"

To his surprise, Chase sensed an answer to his question. It wasn't a verbal communication, just a feeling from within. He turned right and began walking along the road. *I'll take any help I can get.*

As he approached a row of condos, he sensed a fleeting movement from behind him. He twisted around, catching a glimpse of a person with white hair, and then just as quickly he was gone. *An elderly person?* Strange. His feelings of paranoia must be returning. Since his intuition had proven correct last time, he would not ignore it now. He continued walking but remained alert and aware of everything around him.

On closer inspection, the houses and condos looked broken down. The paint was faded and chipping as if these places had not seen a paintbrush in many years. Shutters hung sideways, and yards were overgrown. The Mayor would not be happy with the condition of the houses on this street. He prided himself on the quaint and welcoming atmosphere of their small town and marketed that fact every chance he got. The houses he walked past now did not meet the town ordinance fining any resident if the exterior of their home did not meet regulations.

There was a peculiar eeriness to the silence. Something felt ... off. Chase looked left and right as he walked. The familiar tickle ran down the back of his neck, and he glanced over his shoulder. Nothing. He continued moving. More broken down houses greeted him with each corner he turned. His shoulders drooped as he took in the sight of his town in this state of disrepair.

Up ahead, a movement caught his eye. A curtain in the corner house fluttered, as if someone had been observing him and had let the curtain fall when he looked in that direction. *Strange.* He considered knocking on the door, but decided against it and continued on his quest.

Finally, he recognized a street name, the sign lying on its side by the road, and realized where he was. He began running ahead. As he sprinted, he became aware of a change in his body. All of this running should have made his body feel tired, his heartrate accelerate and his breathing speed up, but instead he was refreshed. He could feel a flow of continuous energy coursing through him, and his breathing and heart rate remained steady. They did not accelerate with the exercise, as was the norm. He stopped to look at his watch and realized that his heartbeat was keeping perfect time with the ticking of the clock. One beat per second. *Interesting.* He continued running in the direction of home, testing his endurance and feeling like Superman. He wished he could communicate with his child-self, who had once wished so fervently to develop a super-power of his own. Chase smiled to himself as he ran.

His eyes landed on a bike, rust eating through the paint, tossed on the side of the road and he decided to 'borrow' it. Despite the bike's outward appearance, the wheels were in surprisingly good shape, and he couldn't contain his excitement at reaching the street on which he had grown up. *There's no place like home.* For the first time, he understood the truth in those words.

He gently laid the bike on its side on the front lawn and stopped in his tracks when his eyes took in the house. It was in the same disrepair as the rest of the town, and Chase hung his head, barely able to look at the neglect. Uncle Charlie would be appalled. His uncle had taken great pride in the condition of the house. He squared his shoulders and walked up to the front door and turned the knob. Locked. Creeping around the side of the house, Chase once again saw the flutter of a curtain from what had been his bedroom on the second floor. The house was not deserted. *Alyx?* With one negative headshake, he dismissed the idea. Alyx would have signaled him somehow. *Ok, so if not Alyx, then who? Could it be Uncle Charlie, alive and well in this dimension?*

The sound of approaching sirens pierced the morning silence, and Chase realized they were stopping in front of the house. He jumped behind the shed and listened as two police officers knocked on the front door. He heard voices, though he could not make out what was said from his vantage point.

The officers sauntered around the house. Chase recognized the guns they carried. Spark guns. After a quick search, they holstered their weapons and returned to their cruiser. It was an odd-looking vehicle, not like police cars from home. It had a sleek, compact body style, with a pointed front end. To Chase, it looked like something from a futuristic movie. He almost expected it to hover above the street, and laughed ironically under his breath when it drove off, wheels rolling on the ground.

The officers gone, Chase emerged from his hiding spot. He approached the back door, and once again turned the knob. A noise from behind him stopped his progress, and he turned to find a child, covered in filth and with snarly hair, staring at him shyly from behind a bush.

"Hi. I'm Chase, what's your name?"

"You shouldn't be here. They'll take you away."

"Who will take me? The police? I haven't broken any laws, so there's no need to worry about the police."

"But you have broken a law. The Curfew. No one's supposed to be outside until 11:00."

"You're outside." Chase pointed out.

"I'm sneaking. I don't think they should be able to tell us what to do and when to eat. I want to make up my own mind. I know I'm not supposed to, but..."

"It's okay. Who are 'they'?"

"The Rulers."

"The Rulers? Like the government? Do you have a president? Is this the United States of America?"

"You're funny. We aren't called that anymore. We haven't been for a long time. Not since the Rulers took over, just after I was born."

"Does someone named Charlie live here?"

"No. My Mom and Dad are Dawn and Bray. I'm Ty."

The conversation came to an abrupt end as the back door banged opened. A man burst out pointing an unfamiliar weapon in Chase's direction.

"Come, Ty," he gestured toward the young boy, then focused on Chase. "What is your business here? I called the police once, and I'll call them again. What do you want with my house, and my son?"

"I'm sorry, sir. I don't want any trouble. I thought my uncle lived here, but I was mistaken. I'm leaving now. It's okay." Chase backed away, hands held in front of him, and edged his way to the bike.

"Don't come back. You'll get my whole family arrested, or worse. I'll get rid of you myself if I have to."

"No, sir, I won't come back. Thank you, sir."

Chase jumped onto the bike and pumped his legs, brows furrowed in thought. What was all that business about 'The Rulers'? *Weird.* He'd known things would be different in each dimension, but he hadn't been prepared for the reality of it. He now had more questions than when he started, he still didn't know Alyx's whereabouts, and was beginning to doubt her presence in this dimension at all.

He knew he had to find shelter somewhere to avoid drawing unnecessary attention. At least until 11:00am when he would blend in. He pedaled the weatherworn bike in the direction of the waterfront. He knew where to go.

When he reached the place where the marina had been, he slammed both feet down on the street and stopped, mouth ajar. The marina as he had known it was gone. In its place was what appeared to be some kind of strange military base. No pleasure cruisers resided here, only ships armed for battle. At least he thought they were battleships. They were unlike any ship he was familiar with. The pointed hull was fashioned as a sister to the police cruiser he had seen earlier. Several huge wind catchers spun in the breeze, their constant movement reflecting the sun's light. What appeared to be various kinds of weapons pointed in every direction surrounding the perimeter of the ship, and Chase thought he saw one move in his direction. *Or is it my imagination?* He put his foot on the pedal. *I need to get out of here.*

Just as he began pushing down with his foot, he noticed an unfamiliar flag flapping in the wind and hesitated. Not the comforting stars and stripes of the good ole' USA. This flag was different. On a white background, three blue stars lined up in a horizontal row in the center, cocked as if preparing to shoot out of a red bow. The stars seemed to represent the arrow ready to fly. Chase stood in the stirrups and pedaled with all his stregth, not looking back. He kept his legs pumping until he was sure no one was following him.

He pedaled in the direction of the Moore's house. In his peripheral vision, and for the second time today, he saw a blur of movement rushing quickly behind a house. Once again he had a vague impression of white hair, and a flowing white shirt before the unknown stalker disappeared.

Who is that? And why is he following me?

CHAPTER 33

Cautiously approaching Mason's house on the bike, he turned a corner and slammed his feet onto the street, stopping dead. There was nothing. The house was gone. Walking amongst the rubble, Chase looked for anything that might be familiar. Failing that, he again mounted the bike and took off. If he could just find a place to hide out before the curfew ended, he could make a plan. He hesitantly approached the Gull Street Bridge, dropped the bike, and walked cautiously toward the underpass.

Though the place seemed deserted at first, he jerked his head at a darting movement behind him. He recognized the eerie sound of desperately whispering voices.

"He has a bag. I wonder what's in it? Do you think he has food in there? Grab the bag. Grab the bag!"

Chase raised up his arms in surrender. "Hey, hey. No need for that. I don't have food. But I can help you find some. Don't come any closer," he warned as two men approached him from either side.

"What's in the bag, boy?"

"Nothing you need to know about. I said back up."

"Now, boy, you know what's going to happen here. Why don't you just toss us the bag, and be on your way."

"No." Until that moment, Chase had focused all of his attention on the man talking. Now, he turned to look at the other man, and though he did not recognize him at first, he soon realized who this man was. "Mr. Moore?"

"H-H-How do you know me? Do I know you?" The man said as he took an involuntary step back upon hearing his name.

"Is Mason here? Where's Mason?" Chase demanded.

"Who are you? Are you working for them? Even if you are, you don't have to be so cruel. We'll do whatever you want."

"Cruel? What do you mean?"

"Mason has been gone a year now. He questioned their authority, publicly, and they killed him. But you know that, don't you? You're with them. Are you here to finish the job? My wife and I don't want any trouble. We just want to live in peace."

While Chase focused his attention on Mr. Moore, the other man took the opportunity to grab the backpack, successfully removing it from his back, and ran off with it grasped in his arms. As Chase made a move in the direction the man had disappeared, another large man came out of the shadows. "That's a pretty watch you have there, boy. I know someone who is looking for a watch. How about you hand it over here all nice like, and I won't have to come and take it off you."

"I'd like to see you try to take this watch off," Chase challenged.

"Be careful Ed," Jean Moore whispered in the man's direction.

The man advanced, and Chase stood his ground. "I don't want any trouble, Ed," Chase spoke quietly. When the man approached and grabbed at the watch, a single arc of electricity burst from the watch and connected the watch to the man's forehead like a static bridge. Ed went down instantly, convulsed once, then lay unmoving. The only evidence of the attack was a small puff of smoke disappearing above Ed's head. Chase cleared his throat and held out his arm.

"I'd like my bag back, please."

"Give him his back his bag, Ben Jones, this boy is trouble." David Moore gestured toward the boy.

The first man, he now knew his name was Ben, slinked out of the shadows, clutching the bag to his chest.

"I don't want any trouble, man. Here's your bag, no harm done."

"I'm going to look through my bag now, Ben, and there better not be anything missing." Chase grabbed the bag and walked a few paces away to check its contents. Satisfied that everything was accounted for, he asked a question to no one in particular, "Who are 'They'? Everyone talks about 'Them' or 'They.' Can you tell me who they are?"

"Where have you been, boy? Under a rock?" Sniggered the first man.

"Um, I've had amnesia, and the last thing I remember is...is...it's not important, I just don't remember much."

Mr. Moore stepped forward, and whispered so quietly Chase wondered if he imagined it, "An evil woman runs the country now. Ursa O'Ryan, and her devil of a husband, Pavo. They took over the White House with some kind of new weapon they invented. They rule by fear. You don't want to cross them. The things they do..."

"David! Don't say anymore. He's a spy. You know what the consequences will be if you betray them. And he's wearing a watch. That's how this all started." There was a collective gasp as Mrs. Moore stepped out of the shadows. She was bone-thin, her face sunken in, her shadowed eyes dull and lifeless. "If they find out we found a boy with a watch and didn't report it, we'll all be dead."

"Ben is already on his way to report him. As soon as his watch killed Ed, Ben returned the backpack and took off."

Chase took one step backward. Then another.

I have to get out of here. But where?

The authorities would arrive any moment to take him away. He couldn't let that happen.

CHAPTER 34

Chase pedaled the bike as fast and as far as he could away from the bridge. Since his body no longer felt the effects of exercise, he could go on like this for hours without ever getting tired. An alarm was sounding in the town, and he knew he didn't have much time. The ear shattering noise of an explosion erupted in the distance behind him, and he could feel the resulting rumble as the street bucked underneath the bike's tires. *The bridge? Why would they blow up the bridge?* He pumped his legs faster.

He wasn't sure where to go. In his world, he knew Dune Harbor like the back of his hand, but here, he was lost. All the places that used to be safe for him were now gone.

As he rode, he thought of Alyx. *Where is she?* If he had to travel the world of dimensions without her, and without knowing what had become of her, he thought he would go crazy. He didn't have any answers. But he didn't have time to dwell on that now; he had to find a place to hide.

He rode past an old gas station. Since he hadn't seen any cars on the road, he assumed the need for gas had become obsolete, at least here in Dune Harbor. He turned around and rode back. Two walls of the building had fallen down, creating a kind of tiny lean-to shelter. Chase made a quick decision and rode into what remained of the gas station's store. He hid the bike underneath the fallen sign that now read 'AWA,' and dug out a space just large enough for his body to fit amongst the rubble. There. He took one long, deep breath and laid his head back on the wall behind him.

The ear-piercing alarm continued to sound throughout the town, making it seem like the war zone it had become. Within minutes, rows of soldiers marched past in the street, clearly searching for something. *Me?* They jerked unfamiliar weapons in every direction as if they, with all of their numbers, were somehow afraid of something. Him? Or their leaders? These skittish men and women did not have the bearing and confidence of typical soldiers. Something was...off.

Chase waited an eternity after the soldiers passed before he moved from his hole. He began searching his temporary 'home.' He dug through the rubble in search of...something...anything...that would be useful for him. He smiled as he picked something out of the rubble. *Jackpot!*

"Ah, I've been waiting for you my whole life," Chase held up the flattened Snickers bar and ripped the paper off. He closed his eyes as he chewed. The chocolate was stale, and pain shot through his molar as he bit down on gravel embedded in the candy. It was the best thing he had ever tasted. He couldn't remember ever being this hungry. Dreaming of a cheeseburger and fries, he continued his search as darkness descended on the town. He briefly considered looking through Uncle Charlie's hidden wooden box that was currently residing in his backpack, but he decided this was not the time. He would wait until he was in a more secure location. It could wait just a bit longer.

Chase spent his first night of dimension Travel sleeping amongst the concrete and rubble. *That's the thing about adventures,* he thought. *They're often only adventures after they're over, and that's only if you manage to survive them.* It's a fine line separating adventure from tragedy. His last thought before he drifted off to sleep was the same as his first thought early that very morning. Had it really only been this morning? It seemed like an eternity.

Alyx.

CHAPTER 35

Alyx was shackled. She had jumped right into the old Marina, only to discover she'd landed right in the middle of the military base. When the soldiers had seen her watch, all Hell had broken loose. When one of them had tried to remove it from her wrist physically, he had been shocked to find out it couldn't be removed. Literally. They had chained her wrists and ankles, and thrown her in the stockade, where she had spent the entire day alone.

Thankfully, the soldiers had kept their distance after witnessing the fate of the last man who had attempted to remove her watch. Throughout the long day, she'd heard whispers about her "deadly watch" and breaking the "Watch Ban" as they spoke in great fear of the mysterious "O'Ryans." They were on their way, and "They would take care of her." They were planning for "her execution" tomorrow evening. *Not if I can help it!*

Where is Chase? She wondered for the millionth time. She hoped he had jumped to a more convenient location, and would momentarily break her out of this prison. Not that she needed a man to take care of her, but it wouldn't hurt just this once. They hadn't mentioned another prisoner, so she clung to the hope that he was safe. *I really managed to bungle this one,* she thought. Nothing was happening as it should. She had thought she was prepared for every possibility. She glanced down at her shackles, arms bloodied from her meager attempts to escape, wrists throbbing from the exertion. She had been prepared for nothing.

And worse, they had confiscated her backpack, which contained all the weapons from various other dimensions. She was breaking Elias Walker's decree to keep the secret at all costs by introducing them to foreign technology. Her ancestors would not approve.

Where are you, Chase? If only they could communicate with each other somehow. An idea blossomed as she stretched her neck to try to see her watch on her shackled wrist behind her back. Maybe they could communicate through their watches. She didn't know if it was possible, but it gave her hope as she lay in her prison cell.

CHAPTER 36

At the sound of a falling rock, Chase jerked upright, instantly alert. Was someone there? He dared not move out of his hole to see, though his arms shook with the need to do just that. After some time passed, he slowly emerged to find a girl asleep on the other side of his wall. He was glad he had donned his sweatshirt during the cool night spent on his bed of concrete, which provided cover for his watch. It seemed to send people around here into a panic, so it was better to keep it hidden.

The girl looked vaguely familiar...

She opened her eyes and jumped to her feet. When he looked into her eyes, he realized it was Ava, the girl he had once flirted with. It all seemed so long ago now. She looked quite different without make-up and her golden tan. Her hair was knotted, and she had a smudge of dirt on her face.

"Ava?"

"How do you know my name? Get back, don't come near me," She had a shard of glass she wielded as a weapon.

"No, no. It's okay, no need for that." Chase held his arms in the air, palms up. "Can you help me? I need help. I'm looking for a girl who has brown hair with purple at the tips. Have you seen her?"

"Why should I help you? You could be an O'Ryan spy, for all I know. Leave me alone." She began backing up.

"Wait, don't go! Maybe we can help each other." He took out a dented can of beans he had found amongst the rubble. "I found food. I'll share it with you in exchange for information."

Chase could almost see Ava salivating at the mere mention of food. Hunger warred with her desire to run. Hunger won.

"Ok." She spoke, her eyes never straying from the can. Using a sharp rock, Chase opened a hole in the can. He scooped beans out with his fingers and handed her the rest. The girl ate as if she hadn't seen food in days. Barely chewing, she stuffed as many beans in her mouth as she could, breathing heavily as she ate. Sauce smeared her lips as she devoured the remaining beans. He looked at the ground.

"So, have you seen the girl with purple-tipped hair?"

"No." She sucked the sauce off her fingers.

"What's going on around here? Why is the town such a mess?"

"Where have you been? Nothing has been the same since the O'Ryans took power. They simultaneously took out the White House and all the State Capital buildings with a new weapon they invented. Once the government was gone and there was no leader, it was surprisingly easy for them to move in. We always thought the United States was invincible, but..." She looked off in the distance as she whispered,

"I was here vacationing with my family, and when the soldiers came in, they killed them all. The hotel was destroyed, and I had no place to go. I've been surviving on whatever I can find, and I try to stay hidden as much as possible. There are others like me. The Rulers initiated a curfew and limited all food and water consumption. The oil and gas supplies ran out. They control everything. With the threat of torture and death for the entire family of anyone who rebels, everyone lives in fear. Why don't you know this?"

"Amnesia."

"Not likely. Well, thanks for the food, but I want to stay hidden for the upcoming execution. I don't want to draw any attention to myself while the O'Ryans are here. If I were you, I'd do the same."

Chase digested this new information as he watched her slink away. He planned to attend the execution to get a good look at the O'Ryans.

CHAPTER 37

Downcast faces filled the streets in what remained of the Town Square. They were here, grudgingly, to witness the public execution. It had been ordered that everyone attend. Soldiers and Police Officers searched every house, and anyone looking to avoid the gathering was shot and killed on the spot. Chase tugged the sleeve of his sweatshirt down over his watch for the hundredth time. He did his best to blend in with the crowd as if he belonged there.

He saw Ty's father, Bray, standing amongst the crowd. Ty peeked out from behind him, protected from seeing what was to come. It didn't take long. The soldiers marched out, holding the arms of the shackled prisoner, whose head was covered by a black bag. The prisoner stumbled, and a guard kicked him in the side. The prisoner fell to his knees, only to be cruelly yanked up again. Even with the threat of death, the prisoner fought back viciously, surely knowing he was doomed to failure. The treatment of the prisoner had Chase clenching his jaw.

His body jerked when a furious vibration emanated from his watch, just as he once again spied the man with white hair moving off in the distance. Following would be impossible in this crowd, and curiosity about his watch won out. He slinked off into the shadows, scanning to see if anyone had noticed. No one was looking in his direction. Raising his sleeve, his eyes widened at the bright glow coming off the watch. Furious vibrations tickled the skin at his wrist, and his eyes scanned the crowd to make sure no one around him could hear the buzz of its vibrations. For the first time, he noticed a tiny round knob protruding from the side of the watch. He tilted his head. *That wasn't there before. I'm sure of it.* Interesting.

The gasp of the crowd drew his attention back to the present, and he pulled his sleeve over his watch again. Two people stepped out onto the platform, wearing black-hooded robes depicting the new flag's symbol. "Thank you all for attending. As you all know, lawbreakers are punished by death. No exceptions. No second chances. This girl," spoken while removing the black bag, "will pay the ultimate price of defiance!"

Chase's sharp intake of breath had his heart stopping. *Alyx.* It was Alyx up there in chains. *No!* They were about to execute Alyx. His Alyx. He didn't think. He began running through the crowd, pushing people out of his way like a linebacker plowing the field. He knew he couldn't get there in time. It would be too late. *No!*

His head pounded, watching in horror as they raised Alyx's left arm, watch in place, into the air for all to see, and placed it onto a table. It took five soldiers to restrain Alyx as simultaneously two things happened: electricity shot out of her watch and she kicked out. The battle raged in front of him, and he was helpless to do anything as he continued bullying his way through throngs of people. Alyx and her watch fought together bravely to the very end. She took out four soldiers in her fight, but eventually, she was restrained as more soldiers came forward to take their place, and once again her arm was held flat against the table. He ran forward as they raised an old-fashioned butcher's cleaver, and brought it down in one fluid motion on her arm just below the elbow, removing it and the watch from her body forever. Blood flowed freely from the stump that had been her arm, and Chase fell to his knees as a soldier shot her in the head with a laser gun, her body falling limply to the ground on the steps below, blood still flowing from her stumped arm and smoke rising from her head. All in a matter of seconds, she was gone.

No! His battered mind rejected what it had witnessed. *No no no no. Not my Alyx.* She couldn't be dead. How could this have happened? How could he have let this happen? He looked up in time to see the woman take down her hood as she held the dismembered arm still wearing the watch high in the air. Raising it above her head, she tilted her head back to drink from the blood still flowing out of the arm. The blood dripped down her chin and ran a gruesome path down her neck, giving her a sinister vampiric aura. Her identity registered in his grief-stricken brain. *The hunter.* Ursa O'Ryan, the Ruler of this new country, was the hunter. He should have known. Violent rage surged through his body, and he moved in the direction of the hunter, murder in his eyes.

He did not see the hand that grabbed out until it was squeezing his arm as it pulled him in the other direction. The mysterious man with white hair. The man that had been stalking him since the jump. He fought against him, but the man had surprising strength, and Chase could not break his hold. He couldn't form a coherent thought, so he blindly followed along behind the man. When they reached a house, the man pulled him inside.

He slapped Chase across the face, "Snap out of it! I need you to focus."

"She's dead. It's my fault. She's dead." The man slapped him again.

"Use your watch, you idiot! Let it guide you. You need to place all of your trust in your watch." The man yanked up Chase's sleeve revealing his watch, which continued to vibrate. He belatedly realized that his watch had been warning him of the hunter's presence, but he had been too stupid to realize that before now. What could he have done differently if he had known?

"Who are you? What do you mean?"

"My identity is of no importance. I'm only going to tell you this one time, so listen carefully. She doesn't have to die. Do you hear me? Let your watch guide you." The man looked behind him suspiciously and ran out the door. When Chase followed close behind, the man had vanished.

CHAPTER 38

Chase looked down, unseeing, at his watch. He was empty inside. Without Alyx, he didn't want to continue on this journey he had begun with her. Eyes squeezed tight, he wished he could just go back home, or curl up and join her in death. He fell to his knees on the floor, arms hanging uselessly by his side.

What had the old man meant? She doesn't have to die? She did die. He would give anything to change what had happened. To un-see what he'd seen. He would trade places with her if he could. If only he had known Alyx was here, and that she was a prisoner. Maybe he could have stopped her death somehow. He wasn't sure how, but maybe.

Why hadn't he realized that the new Rulers were the hunters? It was obvious now, but he hadn't figured it out before. *Stupid!* Now that he thought about it, it made perfect sense. He remembered the good old days of stargazing with Uncle Charlie. Even on an overcast night, the most novice of stargazers could easily see the constellation of Orion's belt shining brightly in the sky.

Orion. The constellation was named after the Greek hunter. Orion the hunter. The O'Ryans; the hunters. One in the same. In hindsight, he couldn't believe his naiveté. The flag should have been another clue. The three stars of Orion's belt, with the bow cocked and ready to let an arrow, or in this case the trio of stars, fly into its intended target. It was brilliant, really, in a morbid sort of way.

His mind kept replaying the execution over and over in his head, as if on a loop. *Alyx.* He couldn't accept that his Alyx was gone. He hung his head and cried for her, tears dripping off his chin. At some point, he fell into an exhausted slumber.

CHAPTER 39

Day three in Dimension 7 began with nightmares. Chase dreamed of the execution. In his dream, he witnessed the macabre scene over and over again. Alyx's blood-soaked body, lying lifeless on the steps of the platform. The hunter, holding her arm up as a trophy, drinking her blood. Each time, more people were executed along with Alyx. The Moore's. Ty and his parents. Ava. Uncle Charlie.

Dream Charlie spoke to him. "Chase, boyo, she doesn't have to die. It's true. Listen to the old man. Listen to your watch. Let it guide you."

Chase awoke quickly. A soothing warmth spread throughout his body. Had Charlie broken through the nightmare to communicate with him? He believed he had, as he had communicated with him in his dream state just after his Coupling. A small glimmer of hope took root. If his uncle said so, it must be true. Charlie had always prided himself on being an honest man. He would try. He could almost hear his uncle's voice saying "Atta boy!"

Okay, so what should I do? He stared down at his watch, hoping for some answer to magically come to him. "Ok, Charlie, what now?" He did not experience a magical epiphany, and frustration surged through him. What was he supposed to do? Why did everyone talk in riddles, instead of coming right out and instructing him? He needed Alyx to help him figure it out. *Alyx.* He paced, mumbling with each step.

His eye was caught by the glint against the small round knob protruding slightly from the side of his watch. On old-time watches, similar knobs had been used to set the time and wind them up. He didn't need to set the time on his watch. It kept perfect time on its own. *So, what is the purpose of this knob, then?* He hesitated. There was only one way to find out. Putting his finger on the knob, he pushed in. Nothing happened. He pulled. Nothing happened. He grasped the knob and turned it a notch. Nothing. *What a waste of time.* He stood up and angrily paced the confines of the empty room. *Don't give up.* He'd never been a quitter. Stopping, he took one deep breath.

Grasping the knob between his thumb and pointer finger, he turned it. This time, the numbers began counting backward. What did that mean? He turned the knob one complete turn, and suddenly the white-haired man magically reappeared out of nowhere in front of him, repeating the same phrase he had previously spoken from the exact same spot, using the exact same words.

"My identity is of no importance. I'm only going to tell you this one time, so listen carefully. She doesn't have to die. Do you hear me? Let your watch guide you." The man looked behind him suspiciously and ran out the door. When Chase followed close behind, the man had vanished.

He stopped in his tracks. *Whoa! Déjà vu? What had just happened?* Had the man returned? He looked at the watch. Wait, a second ago, it had read 8:02am Now it read 7:35pm Had he just...turned back time? Literally? Realization dawned as the meaning of the old man's words began to make sense. *She doesn't have to die!* If he had the power to turn back time, then theoretically he could prevent Alyx's death. *But how?* He would have to be smart about this if he was going to get it right. He didn't know how many chances he would get, so he would need to succeed the first time.

Chase sat down to think. His confidence restored, he brainstormed ideas. He would have little chance of saving her if he turned back to the time right before the execution. How would he get to her and manage to keep both of them alive? He would have to go back farther than that. It was pinpointing the exact moment to return back to that was the key.

CHAPTER 40

Chase spent three indispensable days going over and over his plan. *It's not perfect,* he admitted to himself. He'd planned every last detail down to the minute, but there was no way of knowing how others would react in this alternate reality he was creating. The biggest obstacle was that he didn't know the location where Alyx had entered this world when they had jumped here, or at what point she had been captured. Since Ava had mentioned the execution when they spoke, he only knew Alyx had been captive at that point, but he would need to go back to a time before that to set his plan in motion.

All of his attention had been focused completely on planning, and he clutched his grumbling stomach and realized he hadn't eaten in days. He would need to build up his strength if he wanted to succeed, and the food would be a necessary bargaining chip for what he had in mind later. He set out on a quest for food, unsure where to begin. The obvious places had been scavenged previously, and he didn't want to waste any more time. He thought nostalgically of the grocery stores available twenty-four hours a day back home but put the notion aside. He was here, and that's what he had to work with.

Think of Alyx.

He left the abandoned house he had taken temporary occupancy of through the back door, wondering about the previous owners and their reasons for leaving the house empty. He shook his head. *Focus on the plan. Find food.* His fingers closed around a rock and he slammed it down, breaking the rusty lock on the shed. A quick search revealed nothing edible inside. He did; however, find a shovel. His eyes opened wide as an idea struck. *Yes!* He gathered a bucket, string, and a nail. Using a hammer to bend the nail, he packed it safely away in his pack. He began digging in the dirt. He dug deep into the moist soil as he had dozens of times before, uncovering several fat earthworms. In this state of hunger, he briefly considered frying up the earthworms and eating them, but rejected the idea. He had a bigger plan. When he was satisfied that he had a sufficient amount of worms, he placed them in the front pouch of his bag. Chase headed off in the direction of an old familiar fishing pond and hoped beyond hope that it was still there. The pond had been man-made, built in the well-to-do section of town for the pleasure of vacationers staying in the surrounding condominiums. It would be a long walk, but the reward would be worth the risk of being seen.

He reached his destination by mid-day without raising the alarm. To his immense relief, the pond was where it should be. His luck was turning around. He would take that as a sign of things to come. Though covered with a layer of green algae, he was confident that water signified life. He walked around to the far side and unpacked his assortment of treasures from the shed.

After tying the string onto the bent nail and piercing the worm's abdomen, he cast his line into the pond and waited. And waited. Sitting here by the pond, listening to the sound of birds chirping as the sun warmed his head, Chase thought life seemed almost normal. But reality came crashing back as he thought of Alyx.

He didn't know how long he sat there before there was a slight tug on his line. Chase didn't move. He was an excellent fisherman because of his patience, and because he could sense the proper time to pull back on his line to hook his prey. He waited, and upon feeling a stronger tug, pulled back with all his might. Nothing. He replaced the earthworm and cast his line again. Tug. Tug. Tug.

This time when he pulled back on his line, a largemouth bass came back with the makeshift hook piercing its mouth. *Yes!* In his mind, he could hear Mason saying, "Aw come on, man, how come you catch all the fish?" He smiled wistfully at the memory of past fishing trips. He wished Mason was here with him now. And he yearned for Alyx.

Chase immediately cleaned the fish. He briefly considered completing his mission and returning to the house to cook his catch, but rejected the idea. He didn't have time to waste. He ate the raw fish and continued fishing. After successfully filling the bucket with several largemouth bass and a catfish, Chase stood up with his bucket, turned around, and flinched when he heard a yell.

"Don't move! You're in violation of the Food Ration Law. I'll need to confiscate those fish and see your ID." He began walking toward Chase as he spoke.

Chase dropped the bucket and raised his hands in surrender. "My ID's in my bag, I'll need to get it." He slowly reached into his backpack, feeling around for the familiar cool smoothness of his weapon. As soon as his fingers wrapped around his

.45, he pulled it out and shot the man in the chest before he even had time to register the danger. "Sorry." The man fell to the ground, clutching his chest. "Sorry." Chase reminded himself that he was about to change the events that had led him here, which meant that none of this would have happened anyway. Just as Alyx didn't have to die, this man didn't either.

Even so, he thought it would be best to avoid another confrontation, and he didn't know if the soldier had been alone or if more were on their way right now. He headed in the direction of the beach.

It was time to save Alyx. It was time to change time. Literally. He broke into a run in anticipation of seeing Alyx again.

Beautiful. Whole. And alive.

CHAPTER 41

Chase crouched down inside the shelter of an overturned Lifeguard Stand. If all went according to plan, he wouldn't need the cover for long, but he didn't want to take the risk of discovery before going back through time. He fastened the backpack securely, and put his arm through the handle of the bucket with his right arm and held on tight, the metal digging into his skin. Chase was oblivious to the pain.

He was banking on the fact that since everything on his person had come with him when he had jumped here, the same would be true of time travel. He considered the possibility that he would run into his 'other self' in the past but rejected the idea immediately. He hadn't seen his double the first time he'd turned back time when the old man had reappeared to him at the house, so he assumed it wouldn't happen this time either. If he did run into himself, then the more, the merrier on his quest to rescue Alyx from the hunters. He'd just have to wait and find out.

Chase looked skyward and said a quick prayer, then took one deep breath. He looked at his watch. The shiny knob still protruded invitingly from the side of the watch. Very gently, Chase tried to turn the knob to 7:06am on July 7th. One minute before the jump that had brought him here. He thought if he could go back to a time before they had jumped, maybe he and Alyx could agree on a meeting place once they reached Dimension 7, or that they could somehow merge their jumps and arrive at the same entry point. If only he could prevent Alyx from ever getting captured, he would have altered this reality entirely. Even the pain of jumping was worth repeating if he could save Alyx.

He waited. One minute passed. Then two. Nothing happened. *Just as I thought.* He would have to jump back in time within the boundaries of his current dimension.

Switching to Plan B, he visualized the exact place in which he wished to return, and estimated the time he had been there. He hoped he was right. Alyx's life depended on it. Chase grasped the knob and turned it several quick rotations until the display read 8:45am on July 7th, just one hour and thirty-eight minutes after his arrival here. He thought of the place he wanted to return, held his breath, and waited.

He didn't have to wait long. Within seconds he was transported to Uncle Charlie's house, the house that in this world belonged to Ty and his family. It was like blinking once in one place, and blinking again and you're in another. No pain at all for this kind of travel.

Ok, everything was going according to plan...so far. It was time to put his plan into play. This time he did not walk boldly up to the front door drawing unwanted attention but instead went immediately around to the back to search for Ty. He whispered his name, "Ty. Ty." The boy peeked around the bush and then stepped decisively from behind his cover, his chin jutting out.

"Who are you?" The boy boldly asked.

"I'm Chase, we've met before. I'm a 'Good Guy.' You can trust me, I promise. Go inside and bring out your parents. I mean no harm. Tell them not to call the police; I'm here to help you."

"I live here with my Dad. They took my Mom away to be a soldier in the Military."

"Ok, then please go get Bray, I need to talk to him," Chase was encouraged by the lack of sirens that indicated he had already altered this reality as he knew it. Ty disappeared into the house, and minutes later emerged with his father. Bray once again pointed a weapon in Chase's direction.

"Who are you? Are you a spy for the O'Ryans? I don't want any trouble. Ty didn't mean to break the curfew; he's just a boy. I promise he won't do it again." This was said with a stern look in Ty's direction.

"I'm no spy. My name is Chase, and I think we can help each other. I've brought food. Let's go inside where we can talk in private."

Both pairs of eyes focused on the bucket filled with fresh fish. Chase watched the indecision in Bray's eyes as he warred between feeding his son and breaking the law. To Chase's relief, hunger won. He opened the back door and stood back, still holding his weapon on Chase. "Try anything, and I'll kill you."

Chase entered the kitchen and set his bucket on the floor. "Do you have a pan?"

Bray dug out a frying pan, and Chase got to work preparing the meal. As he cooked over a flame rigged inside an old camp grill, he talked, "I've had amnesia, and I don't remember a lot that's happened in the past few years. I recently woke up, and I'm shocked at what I see. Two evil people have destroyed our great country, and I don't understand it. How could the U.S. be brought to its knees so easily? Why weren't the O'Ryans overpowered and locked away? It doesn't make any sense to me."

Ty didn't take his eyes off the food, and Chase felt pity for him as he compared Ty's childhood to his own back in his home world. He put a dish in front of Ty, and he gobbled the food quickly, as if afraid it would disappear before he could finish it. Bray was more reserved, though obviously just as hungry as his son. Chase was concerned that as soon as they finished eating, he would be forced to leave.

Between ravenous bites of fish, Bray answered, "The answer is simple. Fear. After the mass attack on our government, they gathered a small army. Many houses were seized and loved ones taken to serve in their new military, as they did with Ty's mother, my wife, Dawn. Since the army is made up of loved ones across the states, no one wants to fight against them. The military is threatened on the lives of their families back home, and the families back home are threatened with the lives of loved ones in the military. It's a miserable existence, but the majority will not resist for fear that their family will be tortured and killed. There is no doubt this would be the outcome. At the beginning, they made examples out of anyone showing the slightest sign of rebellion. It was brutal and ugly." He looked off into the distance, deep in thought.

"But you greatly outnumber them. The O'Ryans are only two people, and they can't be everywhere at once. I can't imagine living like this. Everything rationed, people, starving, curfews. It's crazy."

"It may be crazy, but it's our reality now."

"Does it have to be? Why can't you go to the military base and gather all of the reluctant soldiers and band together? The O'Ryans cannot fight against such numbers."

"They have weapons. Alien weapons. We can't fight against their power. And I have Ty to think about."

"What would you say if I told you I, too, have alien weapons? And I'm willing to use them to fight for my country. My old country. You remember what it used to be like, don't you? Let's take back the U.S.A. I'll help you."

"As I said, I have Ty and Dawn to think about. But..." He hesitated and looked away.

"What? Tell me, please!" Chase begged, "I have a loved one, too, and she's in danger right now."

"I've heard whispers from others of an uprising. Just whispers, now, nothing but whispers. They may listen to you. They've already lost everything, so..."

"Tell me. Where can I find these people?"

"I won't tell you that until I talk to them."

"When?"

"I'll see them at the Food Rationing at the old school. We're not supposed to talk to each other, but we have our ways. You'll know by tonight."

"I'll be back tonight, then. I have one more question. Where would a prisoner be held?"

"Could be at the police station, but most likely at the military Base at the dock."

Chase grasped Bray's hand in a quick shake and ruffled Ty's hair. "You stay inside and listen to your Dad, Ty." His eyes cut to Bray's. "I'll be back later. I'm trusting you with my life and my girl's life. Please, please let that trust be warranted." He left through the back door and headed in the direction of the Gull Street Bridge. He pulled his sweatshirt sleeve down further over his watch. He wanted to avoid a repeat of his last visit under the bridge.

CHAPTER 42

Chase approached the bridge cautiously. He had packed the remainder of the cooked fish in his bag and had the spark gun in his hand as he laid the bike on its side and shouted, "I'm not a spy, and I'm not here for trouble. Where's Ben? The Moore's? Ed? Everyone out here, now. If I see anyone take off running, I will shoot you in the back. Understood?"

They slunk out of their hiding places under the bridge, hands raised. He counted twenty total. "Everyone sit down. Sit on your hands and cross your legs. I'm not here for trouble, but I don't want some fool running off and raising the alarm. I need your help."

"Why would we help you?" Spat Ben.

"We can help each other. How many of you have family at the Military base?" No one answered, but several eyes looked at the ground. "I have someone there, too, and I'm going to break her out tonight. Anyone with me?"

The sound of bitter laughter filled the space under the bridge. "You're gonna break her out, you say? Don't you think if it was as easy as that we'd have done it long ago?" Ben sneered. "Go back where you came from, boy, while you still can."

Mr. Moore agreed. "They have weapons like I've never seen before. We don't have a fighting chance against them as long as they have those."

"I have weapons, too." Chase held up his bag. "I know where we can get a weapon that can disintegrate the entire Military Base, but I want to make sure anyone who wants out gets out before I do that."

"Where can you get that? Only they have one of those!" Ed sneered.

"It doesn't matter where, what's important is that I can get it, and I'm on your side. Don't you see? The way you're living is no way to live!" Chase was thankful for all his years of playing sports. He channeled his high school football coach as he spoke. "You have to fight back to reclaim your Country! This country was great once, don't you remember? If you let them continue their rule without a fight, then what's the purpose of this existence at all? It's simply existing, nothing more. Is that what you want?" Chase paused to make eye contact with Mr. Moore before continuing, "A man I used to know always told me 'It's worth the fight if the fight is worth it.' I'm telling you, it's worth it. I'm planning to go around town to gather forces. I need help, but I will go forward with or without you. If you know of anyone who isn't afraid of a battle, spread the word. If you run to report this to the Ruler's Guard, they will drop a bomb on this very bridge and all of you with it. Mark my words, you aren't safe here, and you can't trust anything they tell you. Please. Please. I'm begging for your help. And I have food. The food is a peace offering only. You don't owe me anything as payment except your silence. If you don't want to stand with me, that's your choice. All I'm asking is for your silence in return." He reached into his bag and showed them the remaining cooked fish.

All eyes immediately focused on the bag. The smell of fish filled the air, and several people from the group leaned forward, eyes wide. "You'll have to share it, but at least you'll eat today."

He tossed Mr. Moore the food and saw that Ben was missing from the group. "Where's Ben?" He ran to the other side of the bridge and saw that history was indeed repeating itself. Ben was running, again. Chase raised his spark gun, "Ben! Stop, or I swear I'll shoot!"

"Ben, come back!" Yelled Ed. "Don't do anything stupid!"

Ben glanced back but did not stop. "You'll have to shoot me if you want to stop me," he yelled over his shoulder.

"Your choice." Chase fired. Four sparks made contact simultaneously on various points of Ben's body. Instantly, Ben dropped to the street, stiff as a board. Chase turned to face the group of onlookers, "We have to help each other. We can't do that if we don't trust each other. We can take back our independence, but we have to stick together, and make a plan. Who's with me?"

Mr. Moore stood up and looked at his wife. "For some reason, I trust the boy. I don't know why...but he reminds me of our Mason. What else do we have to lose? We've already lost our son. How much more do we have to lose before we decide it's enough? I'll fight for our old lives back. We should have fought a long time ago. Maybe things would be different." He cleared his throat and nodded in Chase's direction, "I'm in. Tell me what to do."

Ed stepped forward, "I lost my wife, and she was the gentlest soul I'll ever know. She surrendered, but they killed her anyway, in a way no one should have to die. These people are ruthless. I'll fight, too. You're right. This fight is long overdue."

For every one that stepped forward, another stepped back. He would take what he could get, and he'd have to trust that none of the others would betray him. He was putting all his faith in the hands of these desperate strangers. It was a gamble he had to take. He couldn't do this alone.

Chase looked into the eyes of the six men and four women who had just pledged to fight with him. A knot form in his throat, and he swallowed it back. "Thank you, I won't let you down. I promise you. All of you. Do you know of any others that might join us?"

CHAPTER 43

As the Bridge community rallied forces and whatever weapons they could find in preparation for the evening, Chase and David Moore went on foot in search of Ava at the gas station. With no luck, they searched the surrounding area. This area of town appeared deserted.

The two of them cautiously approached a building that in his previous world had been a Souvenir Shop. The sign that now lay sideways on the cement read 'Harbor Souvenirs.' They walked around the building, and at the back loading dock found a small entryway. Ducking down to enter, Chase saw a flash of movement to his left. Though no person stepped forward, Chase sensed he was not alone. He raised his voice to the room at large, "Hello, My name is Chase, and this is David. I know you don't know me, but I'm looking for my friend. Her name is Ava. Does anyone know where I can find her?" Silence greeted him, so he continued. "My girlfriend has been captured and is scheduled for execution. I'm going to break her out tonight, and I need help. We've gathered forces under the Gull Street Bridge, but we could use more." Silence. Chase stood his ground and waited.

One man stepped forward, holding a shard of glass out in front of him. "You know Ava, you say? What do you want with her?"

"I don't want anything. We're friends. I'm gathering a group of men and women to fight against the current state of our government. I know many of you have family that serve in the military against their will, and I want to set them free. I want to set all of you free from this kind of life. But I can't do it alone."

Mr. Moore stepped forward. "Carson. Jean and I are following this boy to the army base tonight. You've known my family for a long time. Our boys grew up together. Now my son is gone, and your son is serving in a military he doesn't believe in. I'm sick of living this way, and I know you are, too. We are putting our trust in this boy, and we believe he can do what he says. He says he can get a weapon similar to the one the O'Ryans have. Imagine what we could do with something like that. And if not, well, then at least we tried. It's worth the fight if the fight is worth it. I'm telling you, it's worth it." Silence followed. Six people stepped forward at Mr. Moore's words, Ava among them. She looked at Chase and said, "I don't know you."

"We met when you were vacationing with your family. Don't you remember?"

"No." Though doubtful, she acknowledged that it was a possibility that she had met him on one of her yearly family vacations to Dune Harbor.

Carson looked at Mr. Moore, "You really trust this boy, David?"

"I do, Carson."

"Okay, then. What do you plan to do?"

CHAPTER 44

Chase left Mr. Moore with their new recruits and returned to the house. Once again, he pedaled around back, and this time knocked lightly on the back door. Ty peered around the curtain, the lock clicked and he stood aside to let Chase enter. Bray entered the kitchen scolding his son, "Ty, you never open the door without asking!"

"But Dad, I looked out the window first..." Ty hung his head.

Bray ruffled his son's hair, "Just get me next time, okay?" Ty shook his head in agreement.

Chase gave a nod to Bray, "Have any luck?"

"Maybe. You've got some people thinking. There are people who will gladly go to their death in battle to fight for the old ways. They've been waiting for this for a long time, and have agreed to meet with you, nothing more, no promises. Here's where to find them. Talk to Nick." He handed a piece of paper to Chase. "Godspeed, son." He squeezed Chase's shoulder. "Now, you need to leave here and don't come back. As I've told you, I have Ty to think about, and I won't take any chances with him. I never saw you, and we never talked. I wish you luck." He opened the back door in an invitation to leave.

Chase nodded in understanding. "Thank you for your help, and for not turning me in. I'll always be grateful to you. No matter what happens." He grasped Bray's hand in a shake, winked at Ty, and exited through the back door.

CHAPTER 45

Chase followed the directions on the paper. They led him to Sunset Beach, he and Mason's favorite hangout spot. A picture of Mason playing volleyball flashed into his mind. He fought the wave of sadness and reminded himself that Mason was alive and well back home.

He scanned the beach for a clue to this man, this Nick's, hideout. There was nothing in view except an overturned lifeboat. He walked the length of the beach with no success and stopped to stare out to sea, breathing in the salty air. The ocean had always had a calming effect on Chase. He had often come to stare out at the ever-changing waves in times of distress. No doctor or pill could have the same soothing results as the constant ebb and flow of the ocean water. Today was no different. The tension slowly eased out of his shoulders as he stood there.

He was well aware that Bray may have sent him on a wild goose chase or worse, into a trap, though he had no choice but to trust the man. He turned his back on the sea and yelled, "Nick! I'm looking for Nick! Bray sent me."

"Do you want to get us all captured and killed?" A man emerged from under the overturned boat.

"Nick?"

"Yes, that's what they call me. Bray told me you'd be coming. Let's get out of sight before we're found. Follow me." He once again disappeared under the boat. He literally disappeared. *What the ... ?* It was going to be a tight fit squeezing two grown men under that small boat. Chase shrugged and followed.

As he approached the boat, he saw for the first time that that the sand underneath had been completely dug out. Wooden beams created stairs leading down, and he noticed the walls were framed out with plywood as he proceeded down the makeshift stairs into the sand passageway. Its narrow opening widened dramatically once inside. A cave the size of a small room had been built under cover of the boat, creating a safe haven in plain view against the elements, as well as the eyes of the Rulers and their followers. As Chase's eyes adjusted to the darkness, he scanned the small space. A group of people, young and old, huddled in this sanctuary. He recognized his old neighbor, Mrs. Ruiz, and his friend, Brian, from school, though they did not reciprocate the familiarity.

"This is some place you've got here." He looked around the room, meeting each of their eyes as he spoke. "I'm Chase. I've been going around town gathering forces to fight against the current government. First, we'll take back our town, and then we'll march on other cities to take back their towns. Finally, we'll take back the United States of America! Tonight, the fight begins right here in Dune Harbor. Who will fight with me?"

"Calm down, boy." Nick spoke, "We don't need a leader, we've already got one. Me. We're all happy to join in a fight, but we have to be smart about it. We've been planning a rebellion for a while now, but these things take time. We were thinking in the next few weeks..."

"I don't have a few weeks! It has to happen tonight. My girlfriend has been captured, and the O'Ryans are planning her execution tomorrow. The O'Ryans are on their way here, to Dune Harbor, now! I'm going to stop that execution, or I'll die trying. There are several men and women standing with me, and we will start this fight tonight. If we can take out one or both of the O'Ryans, then half the battle is won. If you want to be a part of this, it has to be tonight. I will not negotiate that point."

"I don't know...going in blindly tonight will ruin all our careful planning. We have someone on the inside feeding us info, but we have no way of communicating with her before tonight to warn her and the other innocents. No, I don't feel comfortable attacking tonight. We need more time. I'm sorry, you'll have to do this on your own."

"But..."

"I'm sorry. My decision's final. Our hideout here needs to remain a secret. If anyone finds out about our little beach cave here, we'll know where they got their information, understand? Good luck tonight."

"Thank you for your time. I hope you change your mind and join the fight. You'd be much welcomed. Tonight at midnight." Chase left, shoulders slumped.

As he dragged his feet down the beach away from the boat, he heard someone call his name and turned back.

"Wait. I will fight. I'm sick of living in fear. If there's a fight tonight, I want to be a part of it."

Chase recognized Brian from school. "Thanks, Brian."

"How do you know my name?"

"I can't explain it, but we knew each other once. Before our government was overthrown. We went to school together."

Brian nodded in blind acceptance. He'd seen many unfathomable things in recent years, and he would not question this. It rang true to his ears.

"Ok. What now?"

"Now we plan. We will attack at midnight when the moon is bright."

As midnight approached, Chase prayed that everyone would follow through on his or her part of the plan without a hitch. This was their only chance.

I'm coming, Alyx. Hang on just a little longer.

CHAPTER 46

Chase sat and leaned his head back, eyelids fluttering closed. A throbbing pain ached behind his eyes, and he rubbed his temples in a circular motion. *Will the plan work?* He mentally went over their scheme for the thousandth time.

Part one of the attack was all about distractions. Since Chase knew he and his small band of rebels had little chance against the army's numbers, this was the key to their mission's success. Mr. Moore and Carson had been left in charge of planning simultaneous triple distractions to lure both the police force and the army away from the base. Since Carson had a background in explosives, he had been charged with creating the bombs. Once the bombs were detonated, they wouldn't have much time to move in and take control of the army base and free Alyx. Everything needed to go off like clockwork for this plan to succeed.

The targeted locations had been chosen carefully. Everyone wanted to avoid innocent casualties of war. Word had spread quickly throughout the town of the imminent attack, and those who hadn't agreed to fight were safely hidden away inside their houses or shelters to avoid the forthcoming battle. They could only hope that there hadn't been a leak to anyone on the inside.

Chase didn't know their total numbers but was thankful for all of the people risking everything to join the battle. He and everyone involved knew the likelihood of casualties during this fight, but all held to the silent agreement not to talk about it. Chase was humbled by the townspeople's resolve once they made the decision to join forces against the Rulers and this new government. And he pushed aside the guilt.

The planned explosions were to detonate simultaneously from various locations at precisely midnight. Chase patted down the sand where he had just buried his backpack for safe keeping, stood up and glanced at his watch. It read 11:45pm *Time to go.* He and five other strong swimmers, Brian and Ava among them, would be approaching the military base from the water. They would wait until they heard the sounds of retreat, and make their move. His group was to be in place prior to the scheduled explosions so they could surprise those soldiers left behind and overtake them at 12:10am The remaining resistors would attack the base from the dock at the same time.

If all went according to plan, he would be with Alyx and in charge of the army base by 12:30am

. . .

Chase waved his arm in signal, and six people silently entered the water from the beach. They had a short distance to swim before reaching their target location. His watch read 11:48pm

In his peripheral vision, Chase spied movement on the beach just as his arms began pumping. *Have we been found out already?* As they had slaved and planned all day, had there been a traitor among them, just waiting for his or her chance to rat them out? Chase changed direction, swimming back toward shore. He planted his feet deep in the sand, and drew his weapon, aiming at the approaching lone figure. "Freeze! Don't move or I'll shoot!" The pull of the current and the feel of the cold sea waves lapping against his thighs threatened to pull him down, but he held firm.

"Hold your fire, don't shoot!" A man stood still as a statue at the water's edge, hands raised in surrender. "It's me, Bray. I'm coming with you, and I'm a strong swimmer."

"Hey, Bray. Where's Ty?"

"I left him in the beach hideout with an old friend. He'll be taken care of...even if I don't return to him. I understand the risks, but I'm coming to get my Dawn and bring her home one way or another. It's time to stop being a coward and take back what's mine."

"Welcome aboard. We need to get going." Chase stuck his gun into his pants and re-entered the water. Their arms cut easily through the water until they caught up to the others. Back on schedule, they silently waited for Carson and his men to follow through with their part of the plan.

11:53pm

CHAPTER 47

Chase and his crew remained in place, submerged and waiting for the telltale sound of explosions shaking the town. Chase kept a close eye on his watch as it counted down the minutes. He saw the exact moment when Bray noticed the watch he was wearing, and whispered, "Trust me. The watch is nothing to fear. The O'Ryans covet them, and that's why they've been banned. I swear you can trust me."

11:59pm. One minute to go. The last minute seemed like an hour. As the watch ticked to midnight, Chase said to the group "Brace yourselves. Any second now." They collectively held their breath and waited. Nothing happened.

12:01am. Nothing.

12:05am. Nothing.

Chase felt his breathing hitch. *Has something gone wrong?* By 12:10, he was sure of it. *We should have mad a plan C...*
BOOM!
The explosion broke the silence of the night with the force of a wrecking ball, followed in quick succession by a second resounding *BOOM*. They waited for the third that never came. The first two explosions would have to be enough.
"Wait ... not yet ..."
He waited until he heard the sound of panicked voices and running feet before he gave the signal to go. His group of seven climbed out of the water onto the dock behind the base building, water silently dripping onto the wood. The success of their plan was contingent on a skeleton crew inside the base office.
They took out the first guard easily, confiscated his weapon, and entered the building quickly. Bray yelled, "Don't shoot! Don't anybody shoot. Madison, we're

fighting back. Come with us! Help us." He looked at Chase, "She is my friend's sister. Madison, you don't want to be here any more than the others. Where's Dawn?"

"Bray!" She immediately lowered her weapon. "How did you get here?"

"Don't worry about that now, I'll explain later. It's happening. We're fighting back. Who else will join us? We need all the help we can get."

"Do you know of a female prisoner?" Chase demanded.

"Yes, she's down in the brig, and she's heavily guarded." She looked back at Bray, "Are we really doing this?"

At his affirmative headshake, she pointed to the video monitors. "She's down there. I can get you there. Follow me. Bray, Dawn left to investigate the explosions." Chase flattened his hand on the third screen. *Alyx. Thank God, she's okay.* Tears burned his eyes as he saw her lying on a cot, foot swinging off the side of the bed. *I'm coming.* His body filled with renewed energy at the sight of her face.

Madison led them toward the dock ramp onto the battleship, and a group of men approached. Their numbers had grown as soldier after soldier defected to fight with their families. Chase recognized Nick and nodded. "Glad you could make it."

Nick nodded in return, "We could have done this without you, you know. Our plan was already in the works."

"Yes." Chase acknowledged as he ran behind Madison into the bowels of the ship. She used her ID badge to bypass security for them, and he realized they wouldn't have gotten far without her there to aide them. As they ran through the narrow hallways, his mouth turned upward at the thought of seeing Alyx again. He picked up speed and kept moving, legs pumping as fast as possible in the confined space.

His breath came out in a *whoosh* when something struck him from behind. A hard object made contact with his ear, pain exploded, and the resulting ringing shook his equilibrium off center. He froze, head down, hands on his knees. When his vision cleared, he recognized the soldier who had kicked Alyx at the execution, the same one who had shot her in the head. Red blurred his eyes as he relived that moment in a second's time. *I'm going to kill you. You're not getting close to her this time.* He read the name 'Brown' on his uniform before kicking out and connecting with his target's knees. The man went down hard but immediately rolled into action, reaching out and taking Chase down with him. They grappled on the floor, and Brown managed to get Chase into a headlock. The man squeezed his neck until darkness filled his vision with tiny points of light. *No, no, no. I'm passing out. Alyx...* In a flash the realization came that he was powerless to overcome this enemy. With his last seconds of consciousness, he groped around his back for his gun. *This...can't...be...the...end...* Blackness converged on the edge of his vision, the pinpoints of light disappearing, as he continued to search for the weapon with his last moments.

Just as his hand made contact with cool metal, someone ran into Brown from the side. The blackness receded. He reached up to caress his injured neck, and focused on breathing. Recognition dawned. *Brian!* The two rolled around on the floor in a fatal battle. As Chase regained his senses, he heard a sickening crack and looked up just in time to see Brian's lifeless body fall to the floor. Brown ran through a doorway and slammed the lock home with a thud. For just a moment they made eye contact through the small portal window, each conveying his own silent promise to finish what they had started, before taking off in opposite directions.

Chase sped full force in the direction Madison had disappeared, his weapon drawn and ready. He stopped abruptly as he entered yet another long narrow hallway. Up ahead, Bray, Ava, Madison, and the others all stood in a small huddle, arms raised and weapons on the floor, along with two bent and bloodied bodies.

They had reached Alyx's room but had failed to release her from her prison. Chase froze. Two guards were holding his new friends at gunpoint.

"Did you think you could succeed in this plan of yours? The Rulers will not be happy to hear about this poorly planned attack. It's our lucky day. I think we'll be having multiple executions tomorrow. That will be much more fun than just one." He laughed maniacally as his companion agreed.

"Wait. Do you really want to do this? Don't you want to make your own decisions? You have no future with the O'Ryans, can't you see? They'll use you and discard you when they're done with you. You're disposable, man. Join us and have your freedom back." Chase pleaded. As he spoke, the sleeve of his sweatshirt bunched around his watch accentuating its blue glow, immediately drawing the guard's attention.

"He has a watch! Seize him!" The second guard reached for Chase and grabbed at his watch. The watch immediately retaliated with an arc of electricity that jumped from the watch into the center of the man's forehead. He fell to the ground, body smoking.

There was a collective gasp and involuntary step back as everyone witnessed the watch's defensive move. "Don't worry. It only does that if it feels threatened. It's not a danger to you unless you try to separate me and the watch." He approached the group as he spoke, making purposeful eye contact with each as he slowly began counting. "One. Two. Three."

Simultaneously, Chase, Bray, and Madison lurched toward the guard just as he fired a shot. Madison fell to the ground, clutching her midsection. Bray managed to knock the man to the ground, just as the watch emitted a second arc of electricity into the guard as he reached for the watch. He did not get up. Bray jumped off the man quickly, looking down at his own body to make sure the electric shock hadn't also hit him.

Bray ran to Madison and took her hand, "Hold on, Maddy, hold on. I'm gonna get you outta here. I'll take you home to see Aidan."

"Tell Aidan I fought bravely. You have to go, don't wait for me. I'm not gonna make it, Bray, I can feel it." Her head fell back, and her body went limp. Bray hung his head as he gently laid her lifeless body down on the floor.

"Alyx!" Chase banged on the metal door. He heard a muffled response from within. He was so close; he had to get her out of there. Bending down, he ripped the ID card off the dead guard's still smoking body. He swiped the card through the keypad by the door and held his breath. The light flashed green, and the resulting click was like music to his ears. The door opened.

"Alyx!" Chase raced into the room and grabbed her. His lips crashed down onto hers in a quick kiss, and he hugged her to his body as if he never wanted to let go. He breathed in her familiar scent and realized at that moment that he was in love with her. He was never letting her out of his sight again.

"Let go, Chase, what are you doing? Unlock my chains; we have to get out of here. What took you so long?"

Yep. He was in love all right.

CHAPTER 48

While Chase released Alyx from her chains, the hunters were en route to Dune Harbor via helicopter. They had already been in the air when they received the communication regarding the attack on the military base in the small coastal town.

Ursa's nostrils flared and she gritted her teeth so hard her molars hurt. She welcomed the pain. She had been elated when the girl wearing the watch had been captured, and had celebrated as she prepared for her execution. After all these years of waiting impatiently, a watch would finally be in her possession. She knew the blood of the keeper powered the watch, and she needed that blood. She had a theory she'd wanted to test for a long time, but she needed a supply of blood for it to work. She wanted to drain the girl's blood and drink it. All of it. If the keeper's blood flowed through her own veins, maybe she could fool the watch into Coupling with her. Her deepest desire was to have the ability to jump dimensions, and she and Pavo had invested everything into making that happen.

She kicked the interior door of the helicopter as the rage consumed her. Pavo sat silently at her side, controlling his anger much better than she was. Her entire body shook with outraged energy, and she kicked the door again. And again. She would make the townspeople of Dune Harbor pay. What could they do if she dropped a bomb to take out the entire town? Nothing. That would teach them. They would all be dead. The smile did not reach her cold, narrowed eyes.

She sat up straighter in her seat as she realized she couldn't do that. The keeper was still alive in that town, and she needed to take her alive if she ever wanted to test her plan. Furthermore, her other self from the previous dimension had communicated that there was a possibility of two keepers jumping at once for the first time in the known history of dimension travel. With the watch Ban still in effect throughout the country, she was confident that another watch wearer would be reported to them promptly.

Right now, she would focus on locating the girl and worry about a possible second keeper later. Maybe their Dimension 6 counterparts had taken care of the second keeper after all. When last they spoke, the newest keeper hadn't even initiated The Coupling and his time had been running out. It was entirely possible that their 'Other Selves' had prevented The Coupling from happening. She had been unable to communicate with them since the beginning of July, but she was not concerned. Communication between dimensions had its repercussions, so they only communicated with each other when it was absolutely necessary.

Yes, her primary concern was regaining possession of the girl and her watch. She would stop at nothing to make that happen.

CHAPTER 49

Alyx stood back, brows furrowed. She chewed on her fingnail as she watched Chase interacting with the men and women around him as if he'd known them for years. He had bonded with the people here in this dimension, and she wasn't sure that it didn't interfere with keeping dimension travel a secret. He had somehow become their leader, and after less than two full days they all seemed to trust him completely. He had single-handedly incited a rebellion using just his charm, good looks, and ability to communicate. She didn't understand that kind of bonding, and she was not accustomed to dealing with outsiders.

He'd been acting very strangely toward her since freeing her from the brig. He stayed within mere steps of her at all times, and he seemed to need to touch her in small ways every chance he got. A brush of hands, a grasp of her arm, shoulders touching, the feel of his hand at the small of her back. *What is wrong with him?* She jerked her finger out of her mouth, realizing she had chewed off three nails already. *And what is wrong with me? I never bite my nails!*

Bray had radioed the other two battleships anchored in the harbor, and once the soldiers had learned of the rebellion, overtaking both ships had been an easy task. The local soldiers outnumbered the Ruler's Guard ten to one, and once they heard the news, it was a small feat to overtake them and throw the ones who survived into the brig. As with any war, both sides suffered casualties, but the count was low and everyone understood that freedom always paid a high price.

Even so, there was an atmosphere of celebration throughout the town.

Townspeople swarmed the streets and converged on the military base, and all shared food from the ships' supplies.

Alyx walked to the bow of the ship to look up at the night sky, turned around and collided with Chase. She automatically put her hand on his chest to steady her, and he took that as an invitation to wrap his arms around her and hold on tight.

"Ah, Chase? I can't breathe. What is going on with you? Something is different.

Did something happen to you when you jumped? And you've broken the rule! Everyone knows about our watches."

Chase laughed, "Nothing happened to me, but something did happen to you. I haven't broken any rules, Alyx. They know we have watches, but they don't know anything about dimension travel. That secret is safe. I'll explain it all to you later, when we have more privacy, okay?" He bent down and kissed her forehead.

"Stop it! Why do you keep doing things like that?" She pushed away and looked out over the black ocean. *What is he doing to me?* Every time he touched her, she felt her body reluctantly respond. She had to resist this power he seemed to have over her. There was no future for them. She knew that. *But is it so terrible to wish that there could be?*

She frowned. These were dangerous thoughts she was having, and she didn't know how to control them. But control them she would since Chase seemed to have lost his grip on reality.

She managed to keep some distance between them as Chase turned to speak to his new friends. Alyx's chin jutted out and her back stiffened as Ava approached them. Even in her disheveled state, she still held a strong feminine appeal. Though more subtle than before, it was just as appealing to the opposite sex.

"Hi, I'm Ava." She held out her hand for a handshake. Alyx looked down at her outstretched hand and hesitantly reached out to return the shake. "Hi."

"Are you okay? Was it horrible being held captive?"

"No, not so bad. It could have been worse."

"Oh. Good. I wanted to tell you, you have a good man, here. He was relentless in his quest to get to you. I hope you realize how lucky you are to have him."

Alyx blinked. "Uh, sure."

At that moment, a woman burst onto the deck of the ship calling out a man's name. "Bray! Bray! Where's Bray? Have you seen Bray?" Chase ran below deck and found his new friend.

"Someone's looking for you on deck, buddy." Chase pointed.

Bray raced onto the deck of the ship. When he spotted his wife, he ran to her. "Dawn." They wrapped around each other, becoming one in an embrace that spoke a thousand words. The kiss was sweet and whispered its own story of reunited love. Just then, Ty ran onto the deck. They picked him up in a three-way hug creating a family circle. The three of them formed a single unit as they stood together on the deck of the ship, and no one else existed at that moment in time. They disappeared below deck arm in arm, and there wasn't a dry-eyed bystander left on the deck.

Alyx saw Chase rub his eyes before he reached for her. She took a step backward out of his grasp. "I need some space. You're crowding me," she grumbled as she stomped away.

"Better get used to it." Chase whistled as he followed behind her.

CHAPTER 50

Chase managed to break free of the townspeople, and he grabbed Alyx's arm as he walked past her, towing her along as he headed in the direction of the beach. She dug her feet in and tried to yank her arm back, but his grip was unbreakable. Despite her initial protests, he could feel her body relax little by little after putting more distance between her and the crowd. *I need to get her alone.* Their feet sank in the sand as they walked along, and he began talking. As he dropped to his knees and began digging into the cool night sand to retrieve his backpack, he recounted the story of her death.

"What are you talking about, Chase? I did not die. I'm right here. 'Keeper' is not synonymous with 'Immortal'. We can die, and if we do, we stay dead. What you are saying is impossible. Did jumping scramble your brain? I think you have been having hallucinations to escape the pain that comes with jumping, and..."

"No, Alyx let me finish. I'm not hallucinating, and I haven't lost my grip on reality. You were captured, and I saw you executed. I saw it with my own eyes, and I thought my life had ended too. I wish I could un-see it, believe me."

"Okay, so you want me to believe I died. Then how do you explain that I am sitting here, right now, alive and well?"

"I can explain it. I'm just surprised that you don't know the answer already. You're supposed to be my teacher. You should know these things...Watch Survival 101, remember?"

"I do not understand you. Maybe it was a bad dream or something." She tilted her head, and chewed on her thumbnail. "It does sound like something the hunters would do, though. I never considered the possibility that the hunters would have this kind of power in any dimension, none of us did. As soon as I heard the Ruler's names were the O'Ryans, I knew it was them. It is so obvious, if they wanted to remain inconspicuous, they should not have chosen the name of a known hunter."

"Uh, yeah, I figured it out, too. Eventually. But that's not the point. It was real,

Alyx, that's what I'm trying to tell you. She cut off your arm, and that guard, Brown, shot you in the head. She drank your blood, Alyx. It was the most horrifying thing..." He reached for her, but she backed just out of his reach. "Don't back away from me. Please. Just let me hold you for a little while. I need to feel your heartbeat and the warmth of your skin. I've never felt so helpless and terrified in my life. Please, just let me hold you while I tell you the rest of the story."

Alyx reluctantly shook her head, but this time when he put his arms around her, she sighed and leaned awkwardly into him. "Okay, tell me."

Chase closed his eyes and breathed in her scent, feeling content for the first time in days. She fit so perfectly in his arms. Even though it was technically only his second day in Dimension 7, in reality, he had been here for over a week. Exhaustion was taking hold, and he would have been happy to hold her like this forever. And sleep. He needed days of sleep to catch up on all the sleep he had lost.

"After your death, the old man with white hair told me 'She doesn't have to die,' and I figured out that I could turn back time. Why didn't you ever tell me our watches could do that? It would have been nice to know that before this all began."

Alyx jumped to her feet. "What are you talking about? We can't do that, Chase, and you say an old man told you that? Who was he? You know what this means? It means he knows about our watches! This is crazy. If you turned back time, show me how you did it."

Chase pushed up his sleeve to show her the knob that had appeared, and it was gone. The side of the watch that had previously housed the protruding knob was now smooth and shiny as if it had never been there at all.

"It's gone. It was right here, see? And I turned it back to July 7th at 8:45am, and I rallied all the people to attack the military base with me, and we broke you out so that you never really died..." Chase's voice trailed off as he realized how unbelievable it all sounded. "Please, you have to believe me," he begged, staring deeply into her eyes. "I need you to believe me."

"I...I do believe you, Chase. But I have never heard about time travel while jumping. Why did the knob disappear? And who is the old man with white hair? There are a lot of unanswered questions. None of it makes any sense, but if you believe it, then I do too."

"I wish I knew the answers. But it's enough that you believe me." He put his backpack on and put his arm around her.

"Uck! What's that awful smell?" She sniffed the air, "It-It-It's you! It smells...like...like...fish! You stink, Chase!"

Chase barked out a laugh, "Did I mention I went fishing while you were dead? There's the proof. I brought the fish through time with me."

"Fishing? It sounds like I died and you had a relaxing day participating in outdoor sports. And your smelly backpack is the proof, you say? You really are crazy; you know that?"

"Crazy for you," Chase punched her arm as they walked back to the others. "Speaking of food, I'm hungry. Let's go find something to eat."

CHAPTER 51

Chase and Alyx returned to the ship together. He was looking for the Moores, and he called out to various people from the crowd as he passed. Finally, he was pointed toward the dock. He located Mason's parents at the dock, standing shoulder to shoulder, holding hands and looking wistfully out to sea.

"I'm sorry to interrupt. Are you thinking about your son?" Chase put his hand on David's shoulder as he spoke.

"Yes. Mason would have loved to be here for this. He would be proud of us. He wanted to fight back, but we thought to conform, and we believed remaining invisible was the only way to be safe. It hurts to admit he was right all along. If only we would have listened."

"He must have been a brave guy. He was lucky to have you two as his parents. David, we couldn't have pulled this off without you."

"We were the lucky ones. We couldn't have asked for more in a son." Jean Moore wiped her eyes.

Chase cleared his throat. "It's good that everyone has their night to celebrate tonight, they've earned it. But you do realize this was just the beginning, right? This isn't over as long as the O'Ryans are still in power." Chase looked at David Moore as he spoke.

"We need to start planning the next step. If we just stay here, we're providing an easy target for them. We need to march out of this town in the morning. I know no one wants to hear about fighting and war tonight, but we need to gather the men and women and start planning as soon as possible. The O'Ryans most likely know about our little rebellion already. They could drop a bomb any minute and take out this whole town in a heartbeat. They'll make an example out of us to deter any others from rebelling."

David met Chase's eyes and solemnly nodded, acknowledging the truth of his words. "Yes. It's worth the fight if the fight is worth it. I'm not going to ask you where you heard that saying. Inspiring words. I've lived by them. I'll find Carson and talk to him now. Let's gather in the Town Square in an hour to start planning."

Alyx pulled Chase aside, and whispered, "Chase what are you doing? This is not our fight. We should not get involved. The more time we spend with these people, the more chance of them learning the truth. No, we should go our own way now."

"How can you say it's not our fight? I'm not going to just walk away after these people helped me save your life. I owe it to them to fight with them, at least in the time I have left here. And how can we hide when we know the real reason the hunters are doing these things to innocent people? It's all because of us. They want our watches, and they don't care how many people they have to torture and kill to get them. I saw that with my own eyes. I know you're not going to like this, but I think we need to take them out before we leave here."

Alyx broke eye contact. "You are right." She took a backward step as she mumbled, "There is something I did not tell you before. My mission in each dimension during my year of jumping is to assassinate the hunters in each World. I did not know how you would react to that part of the plan, so I chose not to tell you before."

"You didn't tell me? You just decided not to tell me? How could you keep something so important from me after I only agreed to all of this with your promise to tell me everything?" Chase stepped back, putting even more distance between them. For the first time since her rescue, he needed to put space between them.

"I agree we should take the hunters out in this dimension. We don't have a choice here. But if we live to see the other dimensions, I can't condone cold-blooded killing unless there's no other way. But that's not even the point. We agreed to be 100% honest with each other. I trusted you completely, and now I don't know if I still can. Is there anything else you've kept from me?"

At her negative headshake, he turned and stalked away.

CHAPTER 52

Alyx pushed through the crowd gathered in the Town Square, and stood along the outer edges looking in. Her nostrils flared at the combination of body odor and smoke fumes that still lingered from the explosions as her gaze raked over the townspeople; families holding children, couples holding hands, the young helping the old, friends standing side by side. *Unity.*

Chase, David, Carson, Nick, Bray, Dawn and the town's mayor stood in front of the euphoric people. Her eyes followed Chase as he stepped forward and cleared his throat.

"The United States of America began as a country of independence, and tonight you took the first step in winning that back. This is a night to celebrate taking back our freedom! The brave people of this town have accomplished what no other town in our country has." The crowd cheered, whistled, and applauded. Alyx stood motionless as she listened to the speech. "Thank you all for fighting by my side. Many of you don't know me. I'm Chase Walker. I asked for your help, and you gave it. It was my honor to stand with so many brave people. I'll always be grateful. Though we need this night of celebration, we also need to start looking toward the future. The O'Ryans will have heard about our fight by now, and they may be on their way here even as we speak. This is just one battle in the fight for taking our whole country back, one small town at a time if we need to. We need to start planning. Tonight." He stepped back. "Dawn."

Alyx's head turned as Dawn stepped forward, along with a group of four other soldiers. "A message was sent out to the O'Ryans during the battle, and they already know of our rebellion. They've shut off our communication, so we will no longer be privy to military information. However, we do know how they work after being a part of their military for so long, and we have a tentative plan. It's dangerous, but it's a plan. If anyone has a better idea, we would welcome your input."

The ex-soldiers outlined possible plans while the townspeople listened, voicing agreement and doubts. Should they take an offensive or defensive position? Through the following hours, they argued and disagreed on various courses of action. Most agreed on one point. They couldn't stay here. It was the general consensus that it was no longer safe to stay in their town. They were now a target. However, leaving would pose a problem for both the young and the old citizens of Dune Harbor. And where would they go?

Alyx had remained silent throughout the evening's discussions. She took a deep breath, straightened her back, and walked to the front of the crowd.

"Um, Excuse me? I'm...um...Alyx. I-I have an idea that would allow you all to stay right here in the town you love. It would be simple but effective. The O'Ryans are looking for watches, and you all know that I wear one." She held up her arm, the purple glow drawing a gasp from the gathering. "Use me as bait. They will come to try to capture me and take my watch. We just need to set a trap for them when they come to take me."

She felt fingers dig into her arm as Chase retorted, "No. I won't allow it."

"It is not up to you. I make my own decisions." She turned back to the crowd. "This could be your only chance to flush them out and end their tyranny once and for all. I cannot think of a better way to lure them in while keeping all of you as safe as possible. Can you?"

There was a murmur throughout the crowd as the townspeople agreed. Why not risk a stranger instead of a known member of their close-knit community?

Chase pulled her aside and spoke through clenched teeth, his fingers digging into her arm, "I. Won't. Allow it. Do you hear me? It's not happening. I will not stand by helpless as they capture you and execute you again. I couldn't live through that a second time."

Her cheeks reddened and her head began pounding. Through clenched teeth, she snarled, "Let go of me, Chase. I am doing it. You can either help me or get out of my way. You know this is the most logical course of action. Why are you fighting this?"

A man from the crowd called out, "Uh, excuse me? Why can't you just take off the watch and use that as the bait? That way if anything goes wrong, we could just give them your watch. Isn't that better than risking yourself?"

She shook her head as she answered, "No, I won't take it off. It's a family heirloom that holds sentimental value to me. I won't part with my watch."

"What about him?" Another man pointed at Chase. "He has a watch, too, right? Why not use his watch if yours is so valuable?"

"Um." Alyx's eyes widened as she made eye contact with Chase. He stepped forward and answered the man.

"I agree. Use me as bait, not her. For those of you who didn't know it yet, I wear a watch, too. I will not take it off because it represents my freedom. If I take it off, they win. I will volunteer to be the bait that lures the Hun...the O'Ryans here. But I will not accept a plan that puts my girlfriend in danger again. Take it or leave it."

Bray stepped forward and put his hand on Chase's arm. "Do you mind if we have a private town meeting to decide what to do? Can you give us a few minutes?"

Alyx heard his urgent voice whisper, "Yes. Please remember, if you decide to use Alyx, I will leave. I cannot stand by and watch her die if something goes wrong. Please don't ask me to. Could you let Dawn use herself as bait?" She felt his grip on her forearm again and found herself dragged into an abandoned building despite her protests otherwise.

As soon as they were out of sight of the townspeople, Alyx grabbed his arm and twisted it behind his back, pushing his face against the wall. "Do not forget, I can take care of myself. You don't get to speak for me. I do not need a man to fight my battles for me. I do fine on my own." She dropped his arm and paced back and forth in anger. "The nerve, telling me I cannot..."

She was unprepared when Chase grabbed her by the shoulders, spun her around, and kissed her full on the mouth. It was a quick kiss, full of the heat of anger tinged with desperation, but it sent a steamy electric shock from her lips to the tips of her toes. She allowed the contact for seconds only before she pushed him away and flipped him to the ground. "I am not the kind of girl you can just kiss when you get an urge. Go find Ava if that is what you want. Do not do that again."

Lying flat on his back, she growled as Chase put both hands casually behind his head and crossed his legs at the ankles. "I know exactly what kind of girl you are. I notice everything about you. Like the way you tilt your head when you're deep in thought. Or the way your mouth lifts on just one side before you surrender to a laugh...almost as if you're fighting it until all at once it bursts free. I know, because I think I love you, though for the life of me I can't figure out why. And I think you're in love with me, too, but I'm sure you won't admit it. You lied to me, and you argue all the time, but I love you anyway. Don't tell me you didn't feel anything when I kissed you because you'd be lying. I told you, I can't watch you die or get captured again. I can't do it. I won't."

Alyx's sharp intake of breath preceded her response. "Love! Love? Are you out of your mind? We met just weeks ago, buddy, and if you think you have some kind of man-claim on me, you are wrong. People take months, even years, to fall in love. There is no future for us. Don't you get it? I am not your girlfriend. I couldn't be even if I wanted to. Is it not enough that we are friends? We have to spend almost a year together before we go our separate ways, so get with the program. It has to be enough."

He started shaking his head before she finished. "It's not enough. It'll never be enough. And I don't believe it's enough for you either. Have you ever considered that there could be a future for us? Think about it. I do. You can lie to yourself, but your beautiful violet eyes give you away, so I'm not buying it. But fine. I'll play by your rules. For now."

Alyx turned her back on him just as Bray came to the door, "We've reached a decision."

"We're on our way." They walked stiffly back to the front of the crowd together.

The mayor of Dune Harbor reached out his hand for a shake, then addressed Chase, "I'd like to introduce myself to both of you formally. I'm Christopher Harris, mayor of this now free town. I understand we have you to thank for that. We are humbly asking you to help us once again. Your girlfriend's plan is sound. But seeing as we owe you a debt of gratitude for your bravery tonight, out of respect for you, we will not accept her offer. But we will accept yours. If you are truly offering to pose as bait to lure the O'Ryans here, then we accept. It's not without its risks, you understand."

Through a red haze, Alyx heard Chase's answer, "Nice to meet you, Mayor Harris. Thank you. You've made a wise decision, and I'm happy to help in any way I can. I understand the risks, but I've come to trust the residents of this town, and I know they'll do whatever it takes to keep me safe. Now, let's get those bastards!"

As the crowd cheered, Alyx stomped away from the crowd.

• • •

Alyx paced back and forth and kicked the sand. This was not going the way she had planned. As a matter of fact, since the day she had met Chase, nothing had. *Love?* He was crazy if he thought she was in love with him. As if he could bat those baby blue eyes at her and she would fall at his feet. *Impossible.* Most of the time they spent together, she was angry enough to scream. How could someone who made her want to throw inanimate objects love her?

It stung to admit it, but it was true that no one else had ever affected her the way he did. And when he'd kissed her, her traitorous body had definitely responded. She'd felt out of control of her own being. And he had noticed, too. She was sure it would be the same with any number of boys; she merely lacked the experience. It wasn't Chase in particular that had been so exciting, merely the thrill of a first kiss. He wasn't so special. She continued pacing, her feet sinking into the sand creating ruts. She huffed, impatiently pushing her hair behind her ear.

And yet, everybody loved Chase. Naturally, he would assume that she did too. *Arrogant ass.* Of course, this town was no different. Of course, they would take his side over hers, even though the whole plan was her idea to begin with. Kicking the sand again, she cursed. She was more qualified to handle herself in a combat situation, and he should know that. He *did* know that. He was just prejudiced because he didn't want a girl to handle this. It somehow bruised his inflated male ego.

Alyx plopped down in the sand and looked out at the churning waters. She felt the same turmoil swirling inside of her as the sand scattered by the waves. She considered leaving, but rejected the idea. She had to complete the mission. It was her purpose. She couldn't walk away from everything she had trained for her whole life. Unfortunately, killing the hunters was a big part of that plan, so she would just have to stick it out. She would ignore Chase, she decided. Let him goggle at Ava. She didn't want him anyway. He was smothering her.

CHAPTER 53

In fishing, it's important to choose the right hook before dangling the bait. The same was true in fishing for dictators. If you use the wrong hook, the fish will take the bait, but the fisherman will not take the fish. Chase wanted to avoid that happening. It was extremely important that enough information was leaked to the hunters, but not too much to cause suspicion. If the hunters thought they were marching into a trap, they might just cut their losses and blow up the entire town.

The plan was simple. Though the military communications had been cut off, they could still use them to communicate with each other. The general assumption was that the hunter's military could, and would, continue to monitor all frequencies in order to intercept Dune Harbor's plan of action after their recent victory in reclaiming their town. The ex-soldiers would 'innocently' leak the information that a boy wearing a watch was here in the town causing problems. Then they, like all good fishermen, would wait. That was the hardest part. Patience was the key.

It is July 18th. Just three weeks before jumping to the next dimension. Chase spotted Alyx practicing her variation of Yoga on the beach as he had seen her do at their camp in the woods. That seemed like so long ago, and yet it had only been weeks. His heart fluttered in his chest, and he felt his body respond physically as he watched her toned body stretching in unlikely positions. Just thinking about the abrupt kiss they'd shared made his lips burn to do it again and his fingers itch to touch her.

She'd been disappearing a lot in the past few days, and she refused to speak to him at all. At first, he had tried to get through to her, but he was trying to give her the space she seemed to need. He sighed, hands on his hips. He understood her frustration at the town's choice and even her irritation with him in usurping her plan. But enough was enough. He missed her. The recurring nightmare that replayed her execution over and over was killing him.

It didn't help that Ava had taken advantage of their temporary estrangement. Just then, he turned around and bumped into her, though he had been unaware of her presence until that moment. "Uh, sorry." *Great! Just who I wanted to see.* He turned his face to hide his annoyed expression. It wasn't her fault. She meant well, she just...wasn't Alyx. As he watched, Alyx turned around, and her shoulders immediately stiffened when she saw him with Ava. Chase sighed again. He didn't know how to fix this, but he was miserable without her. She obviously had some things to work through on her own, so he was trying to respect her wishes. He really was. But if she didn't come to her senses soon, he would have to help her along.

He admitted he'd pushed her away when he confessed his feelings for her. She hadn't been ready for that, and deep down, he'd known that. If only she knew that he had never said those words to anyone until now. *Until her.* For now, he would need to play along with her idea of 'just being friends.' It was laughable, but if that's what she wanted to fool herself into believing, then that's what he would do. For now. They needed to present a united front in order to defeat the hunters and avoid the current dissension that plagued them.

Chase gave Ava a distracted excuse and approached the beach. "Alyx! Alyx, wait!" He jogged to catch up, and she walked faster. "This is crazy. You are acting like a preschooler. The hunters could attack any day now. We need to be on the same side when that happens."

"You think I don't know what side I am on? Go away, Chase."

"No wait, I said that wrong. I'm sorry. About everything. Really. Please don't keep pushing me away. Forget what I said the other day. We'll just be friends. It's enough. I'll accept that. It was an emotional night, and the lack of sleep must have made me sentimental or something, I don't know. I didn't mean it. I'm sorry."

She huffed out a breath and studied his face. Finally, she whispered, "Okay."

"Okay? That's it? Okay. Well then, okay it is. I guess I can live with okay."

Okay.

CHAPTER 54

The hunters, or Ursa and Pavo O'Ryan as they were known here, were currently residing on a battleship docked just out of view of Dune Harbor.

"Has there been word from our spy? Anything at all?" Ursa fumed.

They awaited word that the girl wearing a watch had been spotted, or word that they could incinerate the entire town if the girl had left the area. Even though they had made acquisition of a watch their life's mission, Ursa was in a mood to destroy. Maybe blowing up the town was the right call, after all. If not for the watch she wouldn't hesitate.

She stopped her pacing to glare out over the water, "What is taking so long? We have been waiting here for days. Days! Someone must know something by now!" Ursa's knuckles were white on the railing of the ship. "Can't you *do* something?" She glared at Pavo.

"What would you have me do? Blow up the town, and the watch with it? If that's what you want, I will give the order now if it will get you to shut up," Pavo glared back. "I'm just as frustrated as you are, you know."

"I doubt that."

The crewmen were keeping a wide berth around the O'Ryans, but Ursa waved the closest man over. "You. Come here. Have we heard any news from Dune Harbor? I'm growing impatient with waiting."

"No, ma'am. No news yet."

Pavo grabbed the man from behind and lifted him with shaking muscles up and over the railing. The man managed a few good punches in the struggle before Pavo roughly threw him overboard. He rubbed his injured cheek and a predatory smile bloomed on his face. "I feel a bit better, how about you?"

She picked up a weapon, took aim at the man in the water, and emptied her weapon into him. "There, that's for hitting you. I may feel just a little better now, too." She smiled for the first time in days. The smile did not reach her eyes.

Another member of the crew slowly crept forward. "Excuse me? Mr. and Mrs. O'Ryan, sir? Ma'am?" Cowering in the face of their dual glares, eyes downcast he quietly continued, "The men have intercepted a communication about a boy with a watch. Nothing at all about a girl. What would you like us to do?"

Ursa's maniacal laughter burst throught the silence, and she clapped her hands together. "So, he *is* here! Well, that's good news. I guess we'll have to blow up another town. Dune Harbor is safe for now. Once we have the watch, maybe two, in our possession, we can obliterate what's left of that wretched town."

Pavo smirked. "How about the neighboring town? I believe it's called Cape Sol. Give the command, soldier. Tell them the order came directly from us. I expect to hear the sweet sound of an explosion rocking that town within the hour. The fine residents of Dune Harbor will hear it, too. I imagine they'll cry for the loss of strangers. Boo-hoo. They're so pathetic."

"How will we get our hands on those watches?"

"Fear and threats, my dear, fear and threats work every time." She grabbed his shirt and jerked him up against her, crushing her lips against his. Death and destruction always excited her.

CHAPTER 55

The ground trembled beneath his feet a split second before the sound of the explosion shattered the silence of the evening. Chase ran into the street, dodging others who sprinted past in mass confusion.

Spotting Bray and Dawn holding Ty, heads tilted back and eyes trained on the sky, he slowly raised his head to follow their gaze. Billowing puffs of grayish-black smoke rose from a mushroom cloud off in the distance, the blue sky a deceptively serene backdrop to the scene in front of him. He took a step back, closing his mouth to ask, "Do you think we were the intended target and they missed?"

Dawn met his eyes with her own haunted ones and slowly shook her head. "No. They wouldn't miss. This was no accident. It's a warning."

"What's in that direction? Do you think it was a populated area?"

"Definitely. They wouldn't waste the ammo. I think they took out another town. Most likely Misty City or Cape Sol. Or both. Anything's possible. They thrive on other people's anguish. I have friends that live in both of those cities." Her eyes welled up as she spoke. "They won't stop until they get what they want. What they want is those watches." She glanced down at Chase's watch.

"Yes." Chase exchanged a meaningful look with Alyx. "What more can we do? Word has been leaked, but there's no way of knowing if they've gotten the info."

"Oh, they got it all right. That's what this is all about." She gestured toward the cloud off in the distance. "Now we have to plan our next move very carefully. Are you ready for the next phase?"

"Absolutely. I was born ready." Contrary to his words, Chase began chewing on his fingernail as he stared off toward the black cloud in the sky. A habit he had broken as a boy.

"Good. And we can track the direction the bomb came from, so we'll know approximately where they are. You have a weapon like theirs, right? Could you take out their ship if we lock onto their location?"

Alyx took a step forward, placing a gentle hand on Dawn's arm as she spoke. "No. There are innocents on that ship as well, just like here. You understand that, Dawn. And besides, we have no way of actually knowing if the O'Ryans are onboard, anyway."

"You're right, I do understand it. It was just a gut reaction to this public display of cruelty. We'll proceed with the plan to use Chase as bait in order to lure them in so we can get a better target. Let's get moving. They're getting impatient, and bad things will continue to happen until they get what they want or take out the entire coast in their quest."

Standing a few feet away and blending with the crowd, the O'Ryan spy slowly slunk away. He'd gotten what he needed. They were using the boy as bait. Now he just had to figure out how to deliver the information. Ben Jones angled his body away from the crowd. He'd failed in his mission when Chase had shot him with a Spark gun under the bridge, but he had no intention of failing a second time.

CHAPTER 56

Chase pushed out the door of the house he and Alyx were sharing with the Moores near the dock. He stretched his arms upward, and leaned side to side. The two of them had reached a tentative compromise, and they'd fallen easily back into their 'friendship'. *At least she's talking to me again.* Her eyes told the truth of her feelings every time she looked at him, even if she wouldn't admit it to herself. He rolled his shoulders and grabbed his towel off the porch chair. *Friends. Ha! Who does she think she's fooling?* But, if he had to choose between spending every day with her as a friend, or not seeing her at all, then he chose friendship. *For now.*

Bounding down the porch steps, he called over his shoulder to Mr. Moore, "I'm heading down to the beach!"

He needed the water. He reached up to squeeze his stiff neck. A swim would loosen the tension of waiting for something to happen. This evening swim had become his nightly ritual. It reminded him of simpler times. *This is for me.*

He stopped to talk to several people along the way, conversing in his friendly manner about the weather, the abundance of food to share, and the temperature of the water for his evening swims.

It is July 25th.

One week had passed since the explosion, and an air of expectancy hung heavily around the town. Some had left the town after this recent attack on a neighboring community, but the majority of the town's population had chosen to remain in Dune Harbor despite the horrific warning sent by the O'Ryans. He had exactly two weeks before the jump to Dimension 8. *Not much time.* Somehow, he would have to make sure it was enough.

The mood of the town was as upbeat as possible under the circumstances, and there was an unspoken, silent agreement to keep banter light and not mention the impending danger ahead. Everyone craved the normalcy they had been lacking for years.

He whistled as he walked at a leisurely pace, his black and white striped beach towel draped over the back of his neck. His watch glinted in the sun, as there was no longer a reason to keep it hidden, and in fact, in his role as the town's bait, he wanted it to be clearly visible to anyone interested.

When he cleared the dunes, he scanned the beach and nodded his head when it appeared deserted. The sounds of the waves reached his ears and the pressures of the past few weeks melted off him like ice cream on a summer day. He had always been drawn to the sea. For as long as he could remember, the sand and sea had called to him, as well as his love and respect for the creatures that resided within. He couldn't see a possible future without the ocean playing a large part in his life. That had been part of the reason he'd had such a hard time picking a college and choosing a career path. Maybe it was why he had fumbled the ball in 'The Game.' He would just as soon captain a charter boat right here in Dune Harbor if it meant he could be on the sea every day. On the rare occasions when he and Uncle Charlie had vacationed away from home, he had felt an inexplicable loss as the miles had separated him from the coast. His Dad had the same love of the ocean, according to Uncle Charlie. At least he shared something with his father since he had never even met the guy.

He toed off his shoes as soon as he reached the sand and dug his feet in. No masseuse could offer the same kind of relief and relaxation. This was free therapy right here. Chase tossed his towel down and threw his shirt on top of it. He entered the water slowly, letting the cold water of the surf soothe not only his body, but also his soul. He closed his eyes and tilted his face toward the sun's rays, a look of contentment bloomed as the warmth penetrated his skin. *Now that's what I'm talkin' about.* The only thing missing from this serene picture of contentedness, was Alyx. He wished she were with him, just simply standing hand in hand in the shallow moving waters of the ocean. He wanted to share this moment, and others like it, with her. *If only she would stop acting so childish and admit her feelings...*No, he would not spoil this moment with his frustrations.

He took off, loping awkwardly through the water, and disappeared underneath a breaking wave. He kicked out beyond the breakers and began swimming parallel to the beach. His body glided through the waves, and his stroke was strong, pulling him easily through the tumultuous waters.

After a few minutes of full speed swimming, his limbs began to tingle and burn, and he reveled in the feeling. Though his heart kept time with the tick of the clock and his body did not tire in the typical way, his muscles did get fatigued, though at a much slower rate than before. He kept swimming until his stroke slowed, and then he turned over onto his back to float on the crests of the passing waves. He lost track of time as he floated until he realized it was time to head back. Turning around, his arms stroked at a more leisurely pace on his return trip.

Just then, something stirred beside him in the waves. A flash of movement to his right had him stopping to tread water. *There!* In his peripheral vision, another movement caught his eye. He spun in a slow circle, eyes searching. Searching. Though he saw no other sign of movement, of one thing he was sure.

He was not alone. Something was keeping him company in the wide expanse of saltwater.

CHAPTER 57

Chase continued treading water. His eyes darted as he searched the whitecaps for any sign of movement. He began pushing himself slowly in the direction of home.

Then he saw it. A triangular silver fin broke the surface of the water, disappearing as quickly as it had appeared. Chase cursed. Keeping his eyes trained in the direction where he had seen the fin, he began swimming with his head out of the water in the direction of home, arms picking up speed. A minute passed. Two. Nothing. But he knew he wasn't alone. *Where is it?*

All at once, an enormous body leaped high into the air a mere fifty feet away from Chase, before once again disappearing beneath the water's surface. He barked out a laugh. *Dolphins!* It was a pod of dolphins coming to investigate this strange person invading their home. Two more dolphins surfaced, and Chase laughed again, splashing the surface with his hand. *Not a shark. Dolphins!*

In no hurry, Chase stopped again to tread water and waited. He didn't have to wait long. A dolphin broke the surface, this time to his left, as another one simultaneously breached to his right. They were swimming in joyous circles all around him, and he laid back to enjoy the show. He began splashing water into the air, and one member of the pod, easily identifiable by the scratches along its flank, came to investigate more closely than the others. It swam just close enough to catch the water in its mouth, out of reach of Chase's touch, and the rapid burst of clicks it emitted imitated laughter. Chase dove beneath the waves, kicking down, and opened his eyes to see the dolphins in their natural habitat. No aquarium on earth could compete with the beauty of this experience. Once again, he thought of Alyx. *Will she believe me when I tell her about this? Or will she laugh at me and think I'm crazy?* A slow smile spread when he pictured her face as he told of this adventure. *Her violet eyes will go all huge, and...*

He jumped when his watch began furiously vibrating, causing a buzzing sound under the water. The smile instantly dropped from his face. He knew the vibrating could only mean one thing. The hunters were near. He would have to think fast if he were to outwit them. He turned in a slow circle, trying to find the source of this warning. *Where are they?* There were no boats visible on the sea, nor were any people within his line of vision on the beach.

Should he turn around and go back the other way? Or continue to swim back to his starting point? The dolphins continued to frolic around him in the water, seemingly unaware of any possible impending danger. They seemed to act as his own personal aquatic escort. The one with the scratches on its side stayed close, immensely curious about the sound and vibrations that the watch made under the water.

What should I do? He'd known they would come after him eventually. *But where are they?* There was no time to ponder the whys and the hows right now. He had to focus on surviving. Lost in thought, he glided along with his new mammalian friends.

As he approached his entry point at Sunset Beach, he reached a decision. He continued his slow pace until he could see his towel and clothing come into view on the sand from his vantage point in the water. The dolphins seemed to sense his mood and were reluctant to leave him as if they could somehow help.

As he turned his body in the direction of the beach, Chase looked down as he felt a frenzy of movement beneath his feet. Something had spooked the dolphins, and they seemed to be in a state of panic. Gone was the atmosphere of excitement, replaced by a frantic unknown fear. The water around him turned crimson, and the red bubbled up and billowed outward spread easily by the current. *Blood?* And then he felt one harsh tug on his leg. *A shark?* He rejected the idea almost immediately. *I don't feel teeth. Can't be a shark.* The dolphins, who had only moments before been circling in a frenzy, suddenly disappeared all at once. The eerie silence that followed was disconcerting.

His watch continued its warning signal, and if anything, the vibrations seemed to intensify. Chase twisted sideways, scanning continuously for a sign of threat. Submerging as he had while playing with the pod, he opened his eyes to meet whatever had grabbed him head-on. At first, the swirling water blurred his vision, but then all at once, he could see two people completely submerged under the water. They wore full scuba gear, and converged on him, aliens in this peaceful environment. It became crystal clear that it was no shark, but a man that had grabbed his leg to pull him under. The men below the surface were more frightening than any creature the ocean had to offer. He was fighting a battle for his life in his beloved sea. *I was so stupid not to consider an attack from* under *the water!*

Then he remembered the blood in the water. Had it been his own? Had he been shot and his brain had not yet registered pain? Reaching down, he blindly felt for a wound on his body and could find none. His eyes followed the source of the red tinted sea and he now saw that one of the dolphins was floating, unmoving on the surface.

Oh no! One of the men must have shot or stabbed the poor animal, and Chase felt a surge of anger so intense his eyes burned with it. He growled and changed his course of action from one of retreat to one of attack. Turning the direction of his body, he swam toward the men instead of away from them. When one of the attackers made a grab for Chase's watch, he turned it toward the man, waiting for the expected electrical arc that did not come. *It must not work under water! Guess I'll have to fight this one on my own.* Chase's head pounded with rage and he welcomed the fight. Craved it.

One of the attackers again grabbed at his leg from behind. Chase gulped a deep breath of air before going under, grappling with the man, reaching out toward his facemask. It the struggle they made eye contact, and he instantly recognized Pavo, the hunter. His anger doubled. Tripled. It was a slow-motion battle, as the water made movement sluggish. He managed to kick his leg free of the man's grip while pushing off and swimming away. He immediately twisted his body around, kicking back toward the man yet again, and this time he made a grab for the man's oxygen tank.

A sudden surge of bubbles surrounded him, his body tingling as if in a whirlpool, as the dolphin pod returned in full force. If possible, it seemed as if their numbers had doubled, and he curled his fingers tightly around the man's mouthpiece. He recognized the dolphin with the scratches on its flank just before it rammed its snout into the hunter's gut. As it rammed Pavo, Chase ripped the oxygen out of his mouth shooting air into the water as the air hose shot back and forth sporadically, nearly hitting him. As the hunter clutched at his midsection, he gulped seawater, aspirating liquid as he tried to breathe.

The second man came to Pavo's aid, offering up his oxygen mask to share his air. The relentless scratched dolphin returned, ramming again and again into various points on Pavo's body. Chase made eye contact with Ben Jones, and his eyes widened as recognition dawned just before Ben pushed off and swam toward the open sea. The pod let him go. They were focusing their attack on one man. *Ben's a traitor! I should have finished him under the bridge.*

He'd heard stories of dolphins coming to the defense of humans in crisis situations, but the stories had always seemed mythical. After experiencing it firsthand, he was in awe. Chase almost felt sorry for their target. *Almost.*

The dolphins continued their frenzied attack for about five minutes, and then disappeared as quickly as they had arrived and the water calmed except for the natural movement of the waves. Only the dolphin with the scratched flank stayed behind. *My protector.* He and his new bodyguard swam slowly toward shore until his friend could go no further into the shallow water. Their eyes met above the waves, the gentle eye looking back at him full of awareness and a primitive intelligence. "Thanks, buddy." Chase croaked as he wiped his eyes. The dolphin swam close enough for Chase to lay his hand on its back, and then it, too, swam away to reunite with its pod. His breath hitched as he turned toward shore.

Chase heard shouting, and looked up to see men running out of the overturned boat's hidden shelter toward the water's edge. *Coulda used the help a little sooner, man.* His friends converged on him as he limped out of the water and collapsed onto the sand. As he sat in the surf, he felt the steady beating of his heart and the ticking of his watch as the waves lapped against his legs.

One hunter gone. One to go.

CHAPTER 58

"Chase, are you okay?"

"Was it a shark attack?"

"What happened?"

Chase's head pounded. The men had been hiding in the shelter as they had every night while he was on his nightly swim. They had been planning their own trap, tossing breadcrumbs of information about the watch wearer's nightly swim at Sunset beach. Chase made sure to go at the same time each night, knowing the men would be in place before he got there. Breadcrumbs. The plan had been to ambush anyone who tried to kidnap Chase in a location away from the town and townspeople. It had obviously worked, only not in their favor. None of them had suspected an ambush from *under* water. *Stupid.* They would have to be smarter next time.

"It was the Hun...Pavo O'Ryan and Ben. Ben was with him. He must have been feeding them information the whole time. They were in full scuba gear, and Ben got away. Pavo is dead. A pod of dolphins killed him."

"Dolphins? Dolphins are friendly, Chase. Are you sure it wasn't sharks?" asked Carson doubtfully.

"Positive. I think I'd know the difference between a dolphin and a shark. This pod of dolphins was helping me. Pavo must have killed one of them, and it was like they were out for revenge. They did not harm me, only Pavo. One even escorted me as far as he could swim with me. It was the most awesome..."

"Are you sure Pavo is dead?" Nick interrupted.

"One hundred percent. There's no chance he survived that attack. The dolphins swam at him full force with their snouts ramming his body multiple times. No one could have survived that attack, and on top of that, I took out his oxygen tank, so he had no way of breathing under the water. His body is out there on the bottom of the sea...a fitting end for him. I wonder if he'll wash up on shore."

All eyes focused on the shoreline as if expecting the body to wash up as they watched.

Alyx ran down the beach at full speed. When she spotted Chase, she stopped and stared at him. He smiled crookedly in her direction, as she slowly approached.

"What happened?" She demanded when she reached him. Her eyes traveled over his body as she took in all of him at once.

"Let's see, where to begin. Pavo attacked me from under water, and a pod of dolphins saved me. He's dead, Alyx."

"A pod of dolphins? He is dead? How did this happen? And how on earth did they know to look for you in the water?"

"It's a long story, and I don't have time to tell it right now. You're not going to like it, and I don't have time to argue with you. Ben was there too, and he got away. He's been spying on us and feeding them information. He must have a boat anchored somewhere near here. His oxygen has to be running low by now. Maybe we can put a group of men together to intercept him before he makes it back to tell the others."

There was a flurry of action as everyone started talking at once. Within minutes, the crowd had dispersed to hunt down Ben.

Ed placed his hand on Chase's arm. "If we find him, let's try to take him alive. Please. I know what he did is wrong, but I'm sure they threatened his family. I'm not making excuses for him, but it could have been any one of us. We all know what it's like to want our families to be safe. He probably felt he didn't have another choice."

There was a solemn murmur of agreement. His words rang true. They would do all they could to take him alive if the situation presented itself. They had another reason for wanting him alive. He could give them inside information about the hunters, aka the O'Ryans. If not, well, he had made his decisions knowing full well what the consequences might be.

"Get some of those binoculars you keep in the hideout. Let's send some men down the beach to keep a lookout along the shore for any small boat nearby. The rest of us, let's get a boat in the water and search from there. They can't be far, most likely they'd have anchored just out of view." Chase looked at Alyx, "Are you coming?"

She nodded. "What can I do?"

CHAPTER 59

Muscles straining, the small group pushed the rowboat into the water and jumped in one at a time. Once they had cleared the breakers, they paddled until their biceps burned, but ignored the pain and kept stroking in the direction Chase thought Ben had gone when he had fled the dolphins.

Scanning with binoculars, he searched the horizon. Without technology to speed the process, they were using their skills alone like seamen of old.

"There! Do you see it? Up ahead, at ten o'clock. Is that a boat?" Chase pointed.

"No, I...wait, yes! I think it is! Paddle faster! We can't let him get back to them!"

The six of them paddled with all of their strength. *If we can capture Ben, we may just have the upper hand.*

As they drew nearer, the small motorboat at first appeared deserted. It wasn't until they were almost on top of it that they saw a body lying face-up on the bottom. He appeared to be dead at first glance, but as they approached Chase realized he could see the chest heaving.

"Ben!" Chase shouted above the sound of churning waters. "Are you okay, Ben?" His only response was to turn his head away. When the boats were side by side, Chase leaped onto Ben's boat. He saw tears tracking down over his ruddy cheek, pooling at his ear.

"Ben. We all understand what you did. Come with us."

With a negative shake of his head, Ben rolled away from him into the fetal position. The torrent of tears and great heaves of his chest continued. "I failed them. Now we're all dead. We're all dead. Dead."

Chase turned to Alyx. "I think he's having a panic attack. Let's get him into our boat and take him home. We aren't safe here. Someone will come looking for him sooner or later, and I don't want to be here when they do."

She and one other man jumped over into Ben's boat. The three of them picked him up, muscles straining. Ben was a big man, but somehow they awkwardly managed to transfer him to their own boat without dropping him. Alyx leaped back over to grab the walkie-talkie lying on the bottom of the boat and tucked it away in her waistband before returning to the rowboat.

As they paddled home, Ben kept up his litany, "We're all dead. It's my fault they're dead. They're dead, and I'm dead. We're all dead."

When they reached the shore, they supported his weight and helped him unwillingly disembark. Chase stood in front of Ben until he made eye contact. "Ben, we all understand why you did what you did. I'm not holding it against you. You hear me? You're not dead yet, and neither are we. They don't know that Pavo is dead, so I guess you're family isn't gone yet, either. Snap out of it and help us. If we act quickly, maybe we can take out Ursa, too. But you need to tell us everything you know. Please. We can save your family, and others. We need your help."

CHAPTER 60

While David and Jean Moore were looking after Ben, Chase and Alyx stepped outside. It had been agreed that if Chase were there, his presence would be a constant reminder to Ben of his own traitorous actions. Ed had arrived, and he was currently trying to reason with Ben. No easy feat in his current condition. The clock was ticking. If they were to keep the element of surprise on their side, they needed to act quickly, before Pavo's death was even discovered.

Alyx turned to face him. "Are you going to tell me now? What happened down there? And how did they find you?"

Chase took a deep breath, "The guys and I set a trap for the hunters. I went down to the beach for a swim every day at the same time, and Dawn and the others casually leaked that information over the radio. The men would hide in the boat hideout on Sunset beach, arriving long before I showed up for my swim so I would appear to be alone. We assumed that if they tried to take me, it would be from the beach or a boat on the water. No one ever considered the possibility that the attack would come from *under* the water. The hunter and Ben were wearing scuba gear, and they would have succeeded if not for the dolphins help. They protected me, and killed Pavo. Ben was with him, Alyx. He was spying for them and feeding them information."

"I figured some of that out during our boat ride. Why didn't you tell me?"

"I don't know. I didn't think you would agree to the plan, and I wasn't going to be swayed. I knew you were not onboard with using me as bait. I guess I took the easy route. I'm sorry. Just remember, you kept information from me, too. It doesn't feel very good, does it?"

"You are right. I'm sorry, and I have been pushing you away. I know I have. I did not mean to, but...I just do not know what to do with you. You make me feel...I don't know. You just make me feel, and it scares me. When I heard that you had been attacked, I..." She looked away. "Can we start over? Let's promise each other right now that there will be no more secrets. Deal?" She reached out her hand for a handshake.

Chase waited until she met his eyes, reached out and held onto her hand with both of his. "Now that's a deal. You make me feel, too, you know." He winked at her, and she blushed. *Blushed? Alyx?*

Just then Ed came to the door. "They have a ship docked just out of view. They have been monitoring our communications as we suspected. And they know about the two of you because Ben told them. He also told them that we were planning to use you as bait."

Chase nodded. He'd assumed as much. "We have to come up with a plan, and quick. We need to act before they do."

"Agreed."

Alyx pulled out the walkie-talkie from the boat. "I think I might have an idea."

CHAPTER 61

Ben spoke into the walkie-talkie he had taken from Alyx, panting as he spoke, "I need to speak directly to Ursa. Now. I got the boy, but Pavo's been kidnapped."

Ursa spoke very slowly and quietly as if she were speaking to a child. "What do you mean Pavo's been kidnapped? How did you let that happen? Where are you?"

"I'm on the boat. It wasn't easy to get away from them. I have the boy with me. I killed him. But Pavo saw some men on the beach and went after them, and they outnumbered him, and they took him down. I didn't know what else to do."

"Come back here. Now. Bring the boy's body with you. Is he still wearing the watch?"

"I-I'm afraid to come back. I know what you'll do to me if I do."

"Do you know what I'll do to your family if you don't? Is he still wearing the watch?"

"Yes."

"Bring him to me. I'll handle the men on the beach."

"I need assurances first."

"You're still breathing aren't you? That's all the assurance you need. I could have torpedoed your little boat out of the water by now if I wanted to hurt you. Just bring the boy to me."

"On my way."

Chase's body lay motionless on the deck of the small boat, a circle of red staining his shirt. Ben started the engine and pointed his boat in the direction of the enemy ship at full throttle.

CHAPTER 62

The skies were tinted a pale, misty blue, and the sea was calm. White fluffy clouds drifted lazily as westerly winds blew gently across the rippling water. By all outward appearances, it was a beautiful day. The perfection was shattered by the man captaining a motorboat that carried a body toward certain death for both himself and his family.

Four military men in a Zodiac intercepted Ben before he reached the ship. As they loaded Ben and Chase's body into the inflatable boat, Ursa barked orders from the deck of the ship. She clasped her hands in anticipation as the boat was pulled up with the boom crane. She had sent a battalion of men to the beach to find Pavo, but her mind wasn't on him right now.

"Can't you make that thing move any faster? Move!" Ursa paced back and forth on deck. Small tremors shook her body with the knowledge that she was mere moments away from getting her hands on a watch at last. She could barely restrain herself from rubbing her hands together in glee.

She looked to her most trusted officer as she spoke, "Officer Wolfe, we'll need to remove the watch from the body by any means necessary. But I have plans for the boy's blood, as well. Do not let a drop of it fall to waste. We'll drain every last bit of it from his body before we toss the corpse to the sharks."

"Yes, ma'am."

"I'll trust no one but you with this task. Understood?"

"Yes, ma'am."

She turned to Officer Brown, "You'll take care of Ben Jones. He will pay for allowing Pavo to be taken. Don't screw this up, Brown. I don't want his death to be an easy one. You can choose the means. I don't care as long as it gets done. And Brown, you won't get another chance if you fail to carry out these orders."

"Yes, ma'am." Brown silently fumed. He'd wanted his chance at the boy, but someone had beaten him to it. He had been looking forward to finishing what they started since the night of the mutiny on the battleship and was frustrated that the chance had been taken from him.

As they cleared the top rail, the officers prepared to disembark from the Zodiac to board the battleship. One had Chase's limp body slung over his shoulder and another restrained Ben's hands behind his back. All eyes were on the two newcomers. No one paid much attention to the officers as they walked with their heads down and averted.

"Bring the boy to me! I need to see the watch." Ursa practically screamed the orders while she stood her ground, never doubting that those surrounding her would do her bidding. Her eyes practically glowed with pleasure. "Be careful not to threaten the watch! It will retaliate if it's still active."

"Uh, Yes, ma'am." Though clearly doubtful, the men moved carefully around the watch.

Ursa could not tear her eyes away from the watch. She tilted her head, "Why is it still glowing? And is it...vibrating?" she asked. At that moment, Chase pushed off from the officer to land in a standing position face to face with her, only twenty feet away. Their eyes locked across the deck.

"Sorry. Not dead. But you are." He brought his right arm around to raise it, his .45 ready to finish her once and for all, when he was sideswiped with a body slam from the left. The force of the hit knocked the gun out of his hand to skid across the deck. Brown charged the moment he'd realized Chase was alive.

In mid-air, he held onto Brown's shoulders in a bear hug, and they landed on the deck together with a grunt. Alyx, in the guise of an officer, kicked Brown in the side, as Bray and Nick, also in officer attire, drew weapons on the remaining officers on the deck. They had overtaken the zodiac after hiding under a tarp on Ben's motorboat, and had given Ursa's officers a choice: Join them or jump ship.

Ursa stood alone, her back to the railing, and sneered, "You thought this pathetic attack would bring you victory? I feel sorry for you. All this hope, so easily crushed. What did you do with my men?"

"You're 'men' jumped off the Zodiac as soon as they smelled resistance. Well, not all of them." The one remaining soldier approached Ursa.

"I've wanted to do this for a long time." He punched her right in the middle of her face, and blood spurted as her nose made a crunching sound. "That's for my daughter. And all the other innocent lives you've taken."

Ursa covered her nose with her hand, blood gushing between her shaking fingers. "You'll pay for that. You'll all pay. You have no chance of winning this fight against my army. All you've managed to do is to give me exactly what I want, times two." She looked meaningfully at each watch.

"Ma'am, a battleship is approaching." All sets of eyes, except three, turned seaward.

Brown, Chase, and Alyx continued to grapple on the deck. Alyx was stronger in hand to hand combat, and Chase let her take the lead, offering support as needed. They worked well as a team, and it took both of them to equal Brown's fighting skills.

When Brown kicked out and caught Alyx behind the knees, she crumbled onto the deck in a heap. Chase decided it was time to end this once and for all. He crawled across the deck to retrieve his .45, took aim, and just as he was about to pull the trigger, they flipped again, and he almost shot Alyx. Sweat beaded on his forehead as he pointed the gun upward, finger off the trigger. After a deep breath, he ran toward the man.

He leaped onto Brown's back, put the gun to his head, and whispered in his ear, "You chose the wrong side." And without hesitation pulled the trigger. Brown fell hard on top of Alyx.

"Get him off me." Alyx rasped.

After rolling Brown's body to the side, Chase scanned the deck. Ursa and her first officer, Wolfe, were gone.

CHAPTER 63

Carson observed the battalion of men invading the beach through binoculars from his hiding place inside the boat hideout. They had been expecting this attack and were prepared for it. He whispered to the men and women with him.

"Since we don't actually have Pavo, we don't have a bargaining chip. But Ursa doesn't know that, and that plays in our favor. Any chance we get, we capture. We do not kill unless there's no other choice. We all know what it's like to want our families to be safe. I'd bet anything most of the soldiers have been coerced into serving. It could be any one of us out there. This is brother fighting brother, sister fighting sister. Remember that." A murmur of agreement rippled through the crowd. He looked at his shoes and cleared his throat before continuing. "And be safe everyone." Carson stretched his hand out to each person, making eye contact with everyone in his small group and offering a heartfelt handshake. "Thank you all. Remember, I go in first alone."

Carson emerged from beneath the boat with his hands raised, and yelled in the soldier's direction, "I'm unarmed. I just want to talk to you. Please, lower your weapons."

Disregarding Carson's words, they all anxiously pointed their weapons in his direction. "Get down, get down!" They stampeded in his direction. "Face in the sand! Don't move!"

"I come in peace. I don't want a fight. I just want to talk. I promise, I mean you no harm. What will it hurt for you to listen to me? I know where Pavo is, and I can lead you to him."

"Get up! Lead us there. Now."

"No. I won't. Not until you listen. Ursa is crazy. You have to know that by now. We can't let her continue to have power. Join us! Now is the time to fight back. If there was ever a time when we could all unite in a common force against the O'Ryans, it is now. It's already begun. We could really use your help."

CHAPTER 64

Alyx's feet pounded the deck in search of Ursa. *We can't let her get away.* If they were going to stop her, they had to take her out now. If she disappeared, they might not have time to find her before the next jump. They had just ten days left before she and Chase would move on to Dimension 8. It was true she had planned to kill the hunters all along, but she was growing rather fond of the people here, and she truly wanted to help them before they left.

She ran down the narrow hallway and stopped. *Which direction?* She jerked at the sound of running footsteps behind her and turned to see Chase. Her body relaxed degree by degree as relief washed over her. *We need to be together. It's as simple as that.* That was why she had refused to be split up when they had planned this sneak attack with Ben. She'd known it was risky to put two watches within Ursa's reach at once. The practical thing to do would have been splitting up. But she'd been practical her whole life, and she was through being practical in matters pertaining to Chase. She held out her hand, and he grasped hers and squeezed.

Together they continued their search. They were a sight. Alyx had a slight limp and Chase a swollen black eye. The results of their scuffle with Brown. But they'd taken him down. Together. *Now we need to find the woman!*

Reaching the seaman's quarters, they entered each room and meticulously searched every corner, with no luck. *Where could she be?* She seemed to have vanished right off the ship. *Impossible. She must be hiding onboard somewhere.* It was a huge ship, with lots of small places to hide. Alyx pictured Ursa cowering underneath a bed somewhere, and a small evil smile curved her mouth upward.

Around them, some soldiers fought, and others surrendered to join the quest for freedom. But still no sign of Ursa, or her officer, Wolfe.

She saw Dawn engaged in battle and stopped to help. *If Dawn is here, that means the battleship has arrived and taken this ship.* They could hear battles fought with words instead of weapons as much as they heard combat sounds. This had been a moment many had prayed would happen, and they were glad to switch sides to join in the uprising against the O'Ryan rule.

Once the battle was over, all who stayed loyal to Ursa were thrown into the brig. There weren't many. Sixteen total. Most of the soldiers on board had joined forces with them and were hell-bent on getting their revenge on Ursa. Bloodlust was in the air.

"I'm only sorry to hear that Pavo is already dead so we can't go after him, too," one man lamented, eliciting nodding heads all around.

Now that the battle had been won, everyone united to join in the search for Ursa. After an extensive search of the ship and still no sign of her, everyone was baffled. She had somehow vanished from the ship. She was gone.

CHAPTER 65

Carson stood on the beach with his newly recruited soldiers. Not one of them had resisted when they heard the news that the ship had been taken. When given the opportunity to fight back, they had embraced it. They now had a united mission: Find Ursa.

Men and women patrolled the beach, searching anywhere it might be possible to hide. Many of them had had to hide in recent years, and they had become very good at it, giving them an advantage in their hunt for hiding places. This was no child's game of hide and seek, but a fatal search for their very lives, and the lives of everyone in this town. And bigger than that, the country. Hopeless people now slowly but surely glowed with the smallest spark of hope after so many desperate years.

"Here! Come take a look at this," a man named Adam called to Carson. Carson turned and headed in that direction.

"What is it?"

"Does this look like footsteps to you? "

"Yes, I think you're right." Carson squatted down to study the double set of fading footprints that led from the waters edge toward the dunes and disappeared.

He called out, "Sound the alarm! She's headed into town!"

Everyone began talking at once and running in opposing directions, scared of actually coming face to face with Ursa while simultaneously yearning for the confrontation. Warring emotions fought against each other, as people made the fateful decision in the blink of an eye. Some ran to hide, while others followed the trail in search of her. Momentary chaos and panic ensued as everyone came to grips with evil entering the town they had fought so hard to save. It was as if one woman with the wave of her hand could destroy humanity. Over the years she had gained a mythical power as if she were infallible. People cowered in fear at just the thought of her. The idea itself was preposterous, but that did not lessen the mutual feeling of despair that enveloped the small group gathered on the beach. The small spark of hope that had sprung to life just moments before, flickered and then began to die away.

Death would follow. They were sure of it. They only waited to hear which innocent lives would be extinguished first.

CHAPTER 66

Chase listened to Carson's static voice on the ship's walkie-talkie. "We think she's in town. We followed her footprints, but we don't know where she is."

"Keep looking!" He threw down the mouthpiece, and turned to search for Alyx. When he didn't see her, he yelled, "Alyx!"

She ran to his side. "I'm here. What is it?"

"Carson thinks Ursa and one of her men are already in the town. They found two sets of footprints."

"Let's go."

They disembarked together and took off at a jog toward the beach. He wanted to talk to Carson and his men and begin a search of all the buildings near the area where the footprints had been seen. *She has to be somewhere nearby, and that seems like the best place to start.*

The shrill sound of an alarm pierced the town, warning the residents to remain inside and lock their doors. There was no sense in looking back and wishing they had evacuated the town as originally planned. Instead, they forged ahead, doing their best to keep everyone in the town as safe as possible.

When they arrived at the beach, Carson jogged over. "I'm sorry, Chase. We haven't been able to find any sign of them other than the footprints. And we've had some deserters. I can't say I blame them. What's left of our group is searching the empty condos nearby. No luck, yet."

"Thanks, Carson. We'll join the search. No apologies necessary. Everyone's doing what they can."

He and Alyx entered one condo after another with no luck. They moved on to beach houses. Nothing. "I don't understand this. Where could she be? Is it possible that the hunters have powers in this dimension?"

"No. As far as I know, the hunters don't have the kind of powers you are talking about. There is something I may not have had a chance to mention to you yet, though. You may need to sit down for this."

"No, thanks. I'll stand. Go on."

"The hunters here are the same hunters that have been in this dimension for the past hundred years. Their ancestor found a way to slow their aging process. Though they can die just like you and I, they do not age at the same rate as us, and they are immune to most diseases. They look like they are in their thirties, when in reality they are much, much older. Not immortal, just very durable."

"Ok. I guess I'm not really surprised about that. Since we're standing here right now in another dimension, I won't question anything you tell me. They can die, that's all I really need to know."

Their heads lifted to listen when they heard the sound of frantic shouting in the distance and ran outside to see what was happening. Whirling gray smoke and blue-orange flames billowed into the air above a Motel a few blocks away. Their legs burned as they raced side by side in the direction of the smoke, and the smell of burning filled their nostrils. Anguished screams filled the air, and then a sudden, eerie silence broken by a woman's heart-wrenching despair.

"Ty! No, not my baby. Ty! Where are you, Ty? Come to Mommy, baby. Ty! Ty." Dawn was on her knees in the street, the smoking building a macabre backdrop.

Chase laid a hand on her shoulder, "Was Ty in the building?"

"No. I don't know where he went. He was right here with me, and then the building went up in flames, and I focused all my attention on the building, and when I turned around, he was gone. Gone. I was gone so long...I can't lose him now." Her eyes glazed over and she began searching once again, screaming, "Ty! Ty! Where are you, baby? Come to Mommy!" She continued her litany as she stumbled through the street.

Chase took Alyx aside and whispered, "Do you think Ursa has him?"

"I think she does, Chase. She may want to use him as a bargaining chip. They must be nearby. I only hope we do not find his body as an example."

"Then we'll keep looking. We can't give up."

They sprinted around to the back of the burning Motel side by side, and Chase almost tripped over three lifeless bodies laying broken in the street. Ursa had definitely been here. The killing had begun. His thoughts turned to innocent Ty. *Where is he, and what does the hunter want with him?*

CHAPTER 67

They started by searching building by building. Bray led the group that searched the area near the Motel where Ty had been taken. It helped that he was doing something. Every time he thought of his innocent son in the hands of that monster, he fought the overpowering urge to fall to his knees, throw back his head, and scream. Instead, he kept searching. And praying. His son was smart. He would survive. He knew he was alive. He just knew. The alternative was unthinkable.

They couldn't have just disappeared, but it seemed as if that was exactly what had happened. The entire community joined in the search. One of their own had been taken right under all of their noses. She couldn't get away with that. They wouldn't let her get away with that.

• • •

After three days of searching, and random bodies turning up in random places, everyone was beginning to lose hope. It was like she was toying with them. People were beginning to believe that the boy was dead, but no one voiced that opinion to Bray or Dawn. Instead, they continued the search. Whether the boy was alive or not, they still needed to find Ursa and Wolfe.

August 1st.

Only one week until the jump, and they were no closer to finding her than before. Chase was feeling the frustration as they continued the search with zero results. He didn't want to leave here without resolving this problem, but it was beginning to look as if that might be the case.

"I can't leave here without knowing what happened to Ty," Chase whispered fiercely.

Alyx stopped walking and looked up at Chase. "We won't have a choice. You know we won't. I don't want to go, either, but we can't stay, Chase."

"It will look like we're deserting them. It's going to look like we ran away, after all this. I wonder if they'll still fight after we're gone, or if they'll just surrender again, like before?"

"I wish I knew. I do not like this any more than you do. We just have to find a way to help before we go. We still have one week."

As he walked through the streets, an idea formed, and Chase began bellowing, "Ursa! I'm here! Come and get me! You don't really want the boy. It's me you want. I'll make a trade. Me for the boy. Meet me at the Town Square with the boy, and I'll come with you willingly."

Chase squeezed Alyx's hand when she grabbed his. He looked into her eyes and nodded as she raised her voice, "How about two watches? Two watches for one boy? You can have both of us if you give the boy back. What could be better than two watches together?"

They continued walking through the streets hand in hand, calling out their challenge over and over throughout the town until their voices cracked, and ended up at the Town Square to wait. This had been a cat and mouse game from the start. It was time to end it, once and for all.

No matter what price they had to pay.

Bray and Dawn were already there, waiting for them. "Thank you." Dawn hugged them both with tears streaming wet tracks down her cheeks that ended in mounrnful drips off her chin. "Thank you."

Chase swallowed the lump in his throat and nodded. "Now we wait. And hope they heard us. If they did, she'll come."

CHAPTER 68

A shot rang out.

Chase's eyes darted in every direction, but he failed to locate the source. "Do you see them?" He whispered to the small group.

"No, but I think it may have come from that direction," Bray pointed to the right. All heads turned to look. As they did, another shot rang out.

"There!" Dawn pointed up to the windows on the third floor of the Municipal Building.

"Either they're a bad shot, or they're just trying to get our attention."

They ducked behind a trio of abandoned cars. Ursa's voice rang out from the window.

"I have the boy. Send both keepers into the building, and we'll send the boy out to you. Only the keepers. If anyone else tries to enter this building, I'll kill the child."

Bray's brows furrowed. "Keepers? I don't know what you mean. What are keepers?" He yelled.

"Don't play dumb with me, remember I have your boy," sneered Ursa.

"I need to know he's okay first," Bray demanded. A minute passed in silence. Then a small voice, "Mommy? Dad?"

"Ty! We're here, baby. Right here. We're coming to get you right now."

Chase leaned closer as Bray whispered, "She's delusional. What are 'keepers'? Do you know what she means?"

"Yes. It's us she wants." He looked at Alyx and nodded. "Ready?"

"Ready."

Together they walked toward the building, hands held high, and cautiously entered through the front door, leaving it open behind them.

Though braced for an attack, no one rushed them as they walked through the room. Desks were turned on their sides, computer screens shattered, and they carefully navigated the debris. Chase motioned toward the 'Stairs' sign, and they moved in that direction. He opened the door and yelled, "I'm coming up. When I get there, you send the boy down. The second keeper will come up once the boy is safe with his family."

He moved to take the first step, but he felt Alyx grip his arm and pull him back. She squeezed, "I will be right up. Do not do anything crazy without me. Wait for me. Please."

Chase placed his hand on top of hers and looked intensely into her eyes, "I'll always wait for you." He squeezed her hand, then pulled back and began ascending the stairs. He was more nervous than when he'd played in the championship football game against his school's rival team. There was much more at stake than a scholarship this time. He thought back to a time, not so long ago, when winning a game had been the most important thing in the world to him. *How naïve I was back then.* It seemed as if an eternity had passed since that long ago all-important game. He felt twenty years older.

His feet stopped when he reached the landing that read '3rd Floor'. Hesitating just a beat to take a deep breath, he pushed the door open with his back while keeping his hands in the air. Wolfe was waiting for him with Ty. Ty ran to Chase and hid behind him. He turned and bent down to eye level, saying, "You're safe now, Ty. Alyx is waiting at the bottom of the stairs to take you to your Mommy and Daddy. Go. Now."

Ty didn't need to be told twice. He raced down the stairs in a blur, while Wolfe approached cautiously. He looked at the watch, making sure to stay on Chase's right side, as far away from it as possible.

"Don't make any sudden moves, or you're dead. Take the watch off."

"I can't take it off. If you want it, you take it off."

Ursa walked through the doorway. "It's a trap, Wolfe. Don't listen to him." She walked closer but kept some distance between them. "Finally. Do you know how long I've been waiting for this? Where's the girl? What's taking so long?" She went to the window, calling out "I'm going to count to ten, and if the second keeper is not here, tell her I'll kill him by ten if she isn't up here. One, two..."

In that instant, the door to the stairs banged open just as Alyx released a Blade Disc. It made contact with Wolfe's forehead, lodging deeply between his eyes as he fell to the floor writhing, and then suddenly went still.

Ursa immediately raised her spark gun and managed to get off a shot before ducking behind a metal filing cabinet. Alyx and Chase made a split second of eye contact before the sparks reached their mark hitting Alyx in four different points at once, and she fell to the floor, immobile.

"Alyx!" He ran to her side. Even knowing that she would wake in a few hours, a blinding rage made his eyes sting with heat and his watch glow a furious blue. He flashed back to the horrific scene he had witnessed of Ursa cutting off Alyx's arm just before her guard shot her in the head. The image was burned into his brain forever. "Now it's just you and me, Ursa. Come on out and see what a keeper can do."

CHAPTER 69

Chase cautiously searched the room where Alyx lay stiff on the floor. He vowed to protect her from the hunter no matter what it took. Step by step he inched toward the file cabinet Ursa had been hiding behind, only to find it vacant.

"How does she keep doing that?" He asked the room at large. When he was absolutely positive that she was no longer in the room with him, he headed toward the stairs. There was no other way down, so that had to be her only escape.

He crept down the stairs, reluctant to leave Alyx but just as determined to catch Ursa. He heard a sudden commotion outside and hurried his pace. When he exited the front door of the building, he saw that it was surrounded by all of his new friends. Bray, Dawn, David and Jean Moore, Ava, Nick, Ed, Carson and his group, all of the people he had come to know so well in such a short time, as well as some he didn't know. Ursa was on her knees in the middle, a multitude of weapons aiming in her direction.

"You can't do this to me!" She screeched. "You'll pay for this, all of you. I won't put up with this kind of treatment. You are just one small group of people. I still have thousands of soldiers loyal to me. When they find out about this, you won't have anywhere left to run." Her eyes bulged and spittle flew from her mouth as she screamed.

Bray walked up behind Ursa and grabbed her hair, pulling her head back. He put a knife to her throat, and whispered "Any last words? You threatened my son. You took my wife. You have to pay for that."

Dawn ran into the circle. "No, Bray. You can't! If you do this, we'll be just as bad as she is. It has to end somewhere. Please, Bray, don't do this." Tears streamed down her face. "Let's lock her up. Let her live out the rest of her days in confinement. That is worse punishment for someone like her."

Bray's hand shook with the force of the war waging in his brain and sweat ran off his forehead and down the side of his face. He clenched his jaw so hard his teeth hurt. In the end, his love for his wife and son won out. He lowered the knife, took a step back, and looked in Chase's direction. "I think Chase should decide what her fate is."

Chase walked up to Ursa and smiled. "I think Dawn is right. She should be locked up for the rest of her days, however many that might be." He leaned closer and whispered for her ears only, "And you'll never get your hands on a watch. All that careful planning and you still don't get to have what you want most. What a shame. I wonder how many years until you die? And I bet your fellow inmates will be happy to see you there." He smiled as he turned to leave, and looked back, "Oh, and my condolences on Pavo's death at the bottom of the ocean. I hope he's enjoying his new role as fish food."

Ursa threw back her head and screamed in total frustration and misery, her bruised and broken nose accentuated against her pale face. Either her greed or her knowledge of defeat took over, and she made one last lunge toward Chase's watch, knowing full well that it was the end. As she grabbed for it, an immediate arc of electricity jumped from the watch directly into her brain, and she fell in her final death throes, body repeatedly convulsing, until one last final surge and then total stillness.

CHAPTER 70

Chase stood on the deck of the ship and watched as Ursa's body flopped into the sea with barely a splash. It floated on the waves for just a few moments before her weighted body sank feet first down into the abyss. He inhaled sharply as one arm raised to the surface as if in a last deseperate plea, fingers eerily rising up out of the water, until they too disappeared into the blue and all that was left of her existence in this world was a flurry of bubbles rising up from her corpse. It was done.

Almost too easy an end for someone so evil.

When he returned to town, Chase carefully carried a still-sleeping Alyx and laid her on a bed in a room with red flowered wallpaper, then lay down next to her, and waited. Her watch softly glowed, casting a violet shadow on the crimson flowers on the wall. He was mesmerized by the flow of her blood through the watch. He stroked her face and held her hand, and occasionally whispered words of love to her that he knew she couldn't hear. She wouldn't want to hear them if she were conscious, but he could let all the feelings out while she was in this slumberous state, unaware of Chase baring his soul to her. There was no doubt in his mind that they were meant to be together, in all ways. And this was not exactly how he had visualized their first time in bed together.

He huffed out a breath and intensely stared, as if this would someone speed her recovery. *She's going to hate that she missed the end.* Her breathing was normal, and her heartbeat was strong, so Chase knew he need only be patient, and she would awaken. She had been out for nearly four and a half hours, so he knew his patience would pay off soon. It only seemed like an eternity.

As she slept on, he stared at her face. Such a strong face, even in sleep, with her hair fanned out on the pillow surrounding her like a dark purple halo. She looked like a princess in a fairy tale. The one where the princess fell asleep, and all she needed was true love's kiss to wake her up. *Snow White? Or was it Sleeping Beauty? Or both?* It didn't really matter. Alyx was more beautiful and strong, and...real than any made-up princess could ever hope to be. He'd learned that fairy tales were imaginary a long time ago. Still, for fun, he leaned over and gently laid his lips on hers.

Within seconds Alyx opened her eyes and looked at Chase with groggy eyes. He blinked. Could it be that his kiss had...? No, just coincidence, he was sure. It was just the timing. Almost five hours had passed since the spark gun had knocked her out. Shaking his head, he pushed himself up on his elbow to look down at her. Her waking had nothing at all to do with his kiss. He couldn't believe he had even considered it, however briefly. What a moronic thought to have. *What is wrong with me? Is this what love does to people?*

She shook her head and jumped immediately out of bed, grasping the headboard for support, "What happened? Why are we here? Where is the hunter? Is Ty okay?"

"Whoa. Sit down. You were shot with a spark gun nearly five hours ago. I've been waiting, impatiently, for you to wake up." He patted the bed next to him. "A lot has happened while you were resting. I've had to do all the work myself. It's a good thing I'm here to take care of you on this trip since you've either been dead or asleep for all the good stuff. I don't know how you'd survive without me." He smiled and winked, anticipating the coming outburst.

To his surprise, she barked out a laugh and punched his arm, dropping to sit on the bed beside him. "Tell me."

Chase wondered if he would ever figure her out. "Ursa's dead and Ty is safe. And of course, you know that Wolfe is dead, too." Chase explained in great detail so she wouldn't feel like she missed anything.

"I cannot believe I did not see her die! Why do I miss all the good things? It is not fair." She smiled at him, and he fell even harder.

"She's been reunited with her partner. They dumped her body in the ocean. I witnessed it. It's almost a shame to darken the peacefulness of the sea with her presence." He paused.

"Now that we have communications back, Dawn and the others are spreading the word to all the battleships about our victory here in Dune Harbor, and letting it be known that the Rulers are both dead. Battles are being fought as we speak. We've done a good thing here, Alyx. We've really made a difference. I'm not saying it's going to be an easy road, but I truly believe that these people will have their country back. Maybe not as it used to be, but maybe a new and improved United

States of America will be born from the ashes. There will be casualties, but in the end, I truly think they are on the road to recovery here. And we helped with that."

Alyx held out her hand, and Chase reached for it. They laid their heads back on the headboard and closed their eyes, falling into an easy silence.

Six days until the jump. *I wonder what it's like in Dimension 8.* Filling the dark of the room with echos of color, both watches glowed peacefully. Within minutes, Chase fell into an exhausted sleep, emitting tiny snores as he breathed.

Roles reversed, Alyx, who had slept enough, watched him as he slumbered.

CHAPTER 71

There was an air of camaraderie throughout the small town of Dune Harbor. Reports filtered in announcing more and more victories in other towns all around the country. In a few instances, fighting wasn't even necessary. People laid down their weapons and returned to their families. Those still loyal to Ursa and Pavo O'Ryan saw that they were outnumbered, and ran. It was the easiest conquest in recorded history, though not without its costs. Many innocent people did pay the ultimate price to regain the freedom of the United States of America, as some saw an opportunity to rule in the O'Ryan's place.

Leaders began stepping forward, and the beginnings of a Democracy were in the works. It would not be easy to restore this country to its former glory, but they were willing to give it everything they had to try. Radio communications were slowly returning, and news from all over the country could be shared. Ally countries were stepping up to give aid and lend a hand, and donations of food, medical supplies, and technology from around the globe were scheduled for delivery.

There was a sense of community and pride in every small step toward regaining their freedom. Everyone was willing to unite and put in the work necessary to keep this country alive after it had been dormant for so many years.

• • •

With three days left until the jump to Dimension 8, Chase found Alyx at the kitchen table and threw a bag at her. "Here. Put this on."

Her hand automatically shot up catching it in mid-air as she said, "What is it?"

"It's a swimming suit. It isn't your style, but it's all I could find. We're going swimming."

"Swimsuit? Swimming? But...I do not know how to swim." She reached into the bag and pulled out a hot-pink and white polka dot thong bikini between two fingers. Her eyes narrowed. "Is this a joke? You think I'm wearing a piece of string to go swimming with you?"

"I was hoping you would." Chase barked out a laugh. "Okay, okay. Try this one, then." He said as he tossed her another bag.

She grumbled as she looked into the bag. A crooked smile spread across her face. "You want me to go swimming in this?" She pulled out an extra large t-shirt that boldly stated 'Life's a Beach', and cut-off jean shorts frayed at the ends.

"Yes. Who says you have to wear a swimsuit? Go change and let's go. We need a relaxing beach day."

"What do you do on a relaxing beach day? Do we even have time for that? I am sure we have a million things we need to do..."

"We have three days until the jump. The hunters are dead, and we've done everything we can here. Go change. I'm going to teach you how to have fun."

"I know how to have fun..." she muttered as she left the room to change into the clothing.

Chase waited, and when she emerged in the black t-shirt that reached almost to her knees, completely covering the shorts she wore underneath, he thought he had never seen a sexier outfit on any supermodel sporting a thong bikini. He tongue went dry and he swallowed. "Uh..."

"Don't say a word. Let's go." She walked out the front door.

"Coming." Chase grabbed two towels and a basket and ran to catch up. The sun was shining, and white feathery clouds drifted lazy patterns across the sky. He could hear the call of seagulls, and the sound of the crashing waves as they neared the beach.

He stopped, head tilted down to look at her. "This is my favorite place, and I want to share it with you. Only you, Alyx."

Alyx looked up, and her eyes met his before darting quickly away again. Her voice was barely a whisper, and he had to lean down to hear her reply. "Thank You."

Continuing on, he spread out the towels, took off his shirt, and threw it on top along with his shoes. He smirked as she averted her eyes from staring at his well-toned abdomen. Chase grabbed her hand and began running toward the water.

"Wait! I told you I cannot swim! I will stay on the sand, while you..." She pulled backward, digging her feet in.

"No way! You're going to swim. I'll teach you." He tugged her along.

Their feet hit the water, and she gasped. "It is cold!"

"Cold? This is warm water around here. You'll get used to it."

"Why would I want to get used to it, when I can just get out?"

"Trust me." He angled his head and smiled over his shoulder. After walking a few steps further, he waited to let her body adjust to the temperature. When the water reached their knees, he squeezed her hand. "Tilt your head back, close your eyes, and let the sun warm your face. There's nothing better."

"Uh. If you say so." She did as he asked. With her eyes closed, she angled her face toward the sun's rays. Chase was distracted by the way her hair blew gently around her neck. He felt the moment she relaxed as her fingers loosened their grip on his hand, and she sighed.

"Nice," she said reverently.

"Isn't it? There's no one else I'd rather be here with than you, Alyx."

They stood there for a few minutes until Alyx felt Chase tug her hand as he headed further into the waves.

"Uh, I think we are far enough."

"Not quite. I want to show you something."

As the water rose higher, he felt her body stiffen fighting against wave after wave. Her fingernails left half-moon indentations on his forearm.

"Trust me," he whispered next to her cheek. He felt the tension slowly leave her body as she relaxed against him.

When the water reached her shoulders, she spoke. "Uh, I think that is far enough, Chase."

"Almost."

He pulled her until they went past the breakers, beyond where she could stand, and Alyx clung to him.

"Kick your legs, keep your head up. That's it. Now float."

· · ·

He showed her how to lay back and glide up and down on the sea. She was tense at first, but after a few attempts, she let the tension go and mastered the art of floating. *I'm floating. This has no purpose except...to be.* A slow smile transformed into a grin. *When have I ever done something for no reason?*

Alyx closed her eyes and savored the feeling. She was beginning to understand why Chase loved the ocean so much. She hadn't felt so relaxed in...well...ever.

She realized that she had not had enough moments like this in her life. Oh, she had not had a bad childhood. She knew her parents loved her, her siblings, and each other, and she hadn't been neglected in any way. She just hadn't had much of a chance to be a kid. They took their ancestry very seriously and lived to protect the legacy, and the honor, of being a family of keepers. When a baby was born with the corresponding birth date, it was their duty to train her for her eighteenth year. Though she did not resent her responsibilities as a keeper, for the first time she understood what she had given up for her destiny, and she was glad to share this moment with Chase.

"Chase? Um. There is no one else I would rather be here with than you, either."

She was fascinated by his dimples as he smiled and pulled her closer. When she realized his intent, she pushed back and rolled her eyes, "That was not an invitation to kiss me."

"Come here."

"No."

Chase pulled until there were mere inches between their faces. Her black t-shirt floated around her like a black cloud, and he fisted his hands in it and yanked her even closer. She could feel every hard line of his body fitted perfectly to hers, and her breath hitched as her body came alive as it never had before. Unhurriedly, giving her the choice, he tilted his head and closed the short distance. Slowly, longingly, he lay his lips on hers. His breath on her lips was erotic and sent shivers down her spine. On one sharp intake of breath, her mind went blank. For a brief moment, she allowed the contact and fell into the kiss as it became more urgent. When she thought she would go insane with the pleasure of it, she put her hands on his shoulders and dunked him under the water. He came up sputtering.

"Now you're in for it." He laughed like a child as he splashed water in her face. When he dunked her, she came up coughing. "You have to remember to hold your breath," he said before she found herself submerged again. Underwater, she twisted, grabbed his leg, and yanked him down with her.

They played like children, and when at last they stumbled out of the water, they fell exhausted onto their towels. Time was irrelevant as they basked in the warm glow of the sun, side by side in perfect harmony.

Alyx sat up and stared out over the vast expanse of ocean. "It is beautiful. I never realized. It just goes on and on. I can see why you love it. Thank you for sharing this with me."

"I lo...uh, you're welcome," Chase answered.

"Look!" Chase pointed out toward the sea, and her eyes followed. "Wait, keep looking and wait. You'll see." A minute passed, and a dolphin jumped out of the water and spun before disappearing beneath the waves. Another followed, and several small clusters of fins appeared off in the distance as the pod traveled together along the shoreline, just as they had done the day they'd saved Chase from Ben and the hunter.

"I wonder if that's my pod," Chase murmured. "The one that saved me."

They sat companionably together and watched until the dolphins swam out of sight. "You swam with those creatures? And you were not scared?"

"Nope. It was exhilarating. Man was the only scary creature in the ocean that day."

"Well, I think I will just enjoy watching them from afar, thank you." She laughed.

"Ever built a sand castle?"

"No."

"Perfect. Watch and learn." He began packing the sand in a cup he had brought along just for this purpose.

With a crooked sand castle next to them, and the sun just beginning its nightly descent, they ate a packed dinner together on the beach, just the two of them, and talked about anything that came to their minds.

It was a perfect day. And a perfect first date.

CHAPTER 72

Another day passed. August sixth. Two days until the jump. Alyx was starting to obsess about it.

"Do you have all your weapons?"

"Check."

"I have mine, too. What else have you got in your backpack?"

Chase picked up his backpack and began emptying it. He held each item up for her inspection. The last item in the bag was Uncle Charlie's hidden box.

"I'd almost forgotten about this. We never had time to look through it. Let's check it out."

"I cannot believe we forgot about the box! I am dying to know what is inside."

He unlatched it, and slowly lifted the lid. He inhaled sharply.

"Is that...money?"

"I'm not sure. Yes, I think it is. I wonder if it is real? I have never seen currency that looked like that."

Chase reached into the box and pulled out several different stacks of money, each stack in an envelope labeled with a number. There were seven in all. Some stacks were identical, and others foreign.

"I think it is money from each dimension! This will be useful in future dimensions. I don't see how it would have made a difference here, but it could solve a lot of problems for us on future jumps. I wonder why there are only seven?" He looked at his watch. "Thanks, Uncle Charlie."

"My parents do not have a box like this. I wonder if it is because you are from the bloodline of Elias Walker? It does not matter. You are right. It will be useful. What else is in there?"

"Some kind of yellow gemstone." He held it up to the light, and when the sun hit it, light bounced off the walls in every direction like a sunburst. It was warm to the touch.

"It is pretty. I wonder what purpose it has, and why it was important enough to keep hidden in a wall?"

"I wish I knew." He carefully placed the stone next to the stacks of money and continued looking through the box. He picked up a vial filled with a dark red fluid.

"Uh, do you think that's blood? That's disgusting."

"It sure does look like it." Alyx held her hand out to inspect the vial closer.

"What could we possibly need this for? And whose blood is it? This box is not giving us any answers. It's just posing more questions."

"Do you think it could be...I don't know...the blood of your ancestor, Elias Walker? The original keeper's blood?"

"Maybe. But what good is it if we don't know what to do with it?"

"Good question."

Chase placed the vial next to the other items and looked into the box once again. He pulled out an old, tattered notebook. Meeting her eyes, he opened the book. On the first page, written in an old script, there was a list of twelve names, each with a number next to it.

"I think this is a list of all the original keepers! Did you know all of this?"

"No. We knew your name because it is the same as Elias Walker. That's how my family found you, and we knew one or two others, but not a complete list like this one. This will help us find the third remaining watch!"

They stared at the list:

Walker, 6

Roberts, 7

Apollo, 8

Young, 9

Gray, 10

Vega, 11

Cook, 12

Graham, 1

Woods, 2

Fox, 3

Eris, 4

Atlas, 5

Chase flipped to the next page. "Holy Crap! This is a journal, and I think it was written by Elias Walker!" He skimmed through the pages.

"It will take us forever to read through all of this."

Just then, Bray entered through the front door. Chase quickly threw everything back into the box and slammed the lid.

"Am I interrupting something?" Bray asked.

"No, nothing that can't wait. What's up?"

"Well, Ty's been having nightmares about Ursa O'Ryan, and I thought maybe if you talked to him, he'd feel a bit better. Dawn and I have tried and tried, but he still seems to think she'll come back any moment looking for him. He trusts you, Chase. Can you talk to him?"

"Sure, lead the way."

Bray walked the short distance to his house with Chase on his heels. It was strange not to think of this house as Uncle Charlie's house. He had secretly hoped to find Uncle Charlie in the next dimension alive and well, and living in this house. If it couldn't be his uncle, he was glad that it was a nice family in his place. Ty reminded him of himself as a boy growing up here.

When Bray and Chase walked in the door, Ty ran straight to Chase.

"Hi, Chase. I thought you left us." Chase's heart cracked just a little bit knowing he would have to do that very soon. Children seemed to have a sixth sense about these things.

"Nope, I'm still here, buddy. Want to have a catch?"

"Have what? Is something missing, and we have to go catch it?"

He smiled. It struck Chase that Ty had grown up in a world with curfews, dictators, and scare tactics. He had not had the chance to have a normal childhood, despite Bray and Dawn showering him with their love.

"Do you have a ball?"

"Sort of." Ty's feet pounded up the stairs and back again, his hand clutching a pillow his mother had sewn for him.

"My Mom made this ball for me. I sleep with it."

"That'll do. Bring it outside."

The two walked into the yard, and Chase modeled how to throw the ball back and forth to each other. "This is called having a catch. In baseball, the pitcher throws the ball, and the hitter hits it with a bat, and then he runs the bases and tries to score. A baseball is hard, and a bit smaller than your ball."

Ty scrunched his face in total concentration. "My Dad told me stories about baseball, too. I wish I could play baseball."

"Maybe you will be able to, soon. Now that Ursa and Pavo are both dead. You know you're safe from them, right? They can't hurt you anymore, Ty."

"But how do you know they're dead? What if they come back?"

"They won't come back. Ever. I promise. I saw both of them die. I wouldn't tell you that if it weren't true, Ty. They're never coming back."

"You're brave, Chase. You walked right in there, and you saved me. I don't think I could be that brave for someone else. I was just scared, and I didn't know what to do."

"Yes, you could, buddy. I was scared to death when I went in there, too. Do you know how brave you were when you were held captive? You did everything she told you to, and you stayed alive. That's about the bravest thing I can think of. Being brave is almost always scary. It's doing it anyway that makes you brave, even though you *are* scared."

"I dream about her. She's coming to steal me out of my bed and take me away forever."

"She won't. She can't. I promise you. She is dead. I killed her, Ty. Well, my watch did. She was electrocuted, and her body was thrown into the ocean. I saw her sink into the ocean. She can't hurt you anymore."

"Well, if you say so, I believe you, Chase. I want to be like you when I grow up."

"Aww, Ty, that's about the nicest thing anyone has ever said to me. Thank you for the compliment. You're a tough little guy. You know that? *I* want to be like *you* when I grow up."

"When you grow up? You're already old, Chase." They laughed together and had a companionable catch with a homemade stuffed ball.

When they finished, Chase bent down to eye level. "Ty, there's something I need to tell you. I'm going to have to leave soon. I wish I could stay here, but I have something I need to do. I don't really want to do it, but other people are relying on me, so I know I have to. I can't tell you any more than that. I don't want you to worry about me, and I don't want you to be sad when I'm gone. Keep being brave, especially when you're scared. You're lucky you have two parents who love you very much. They will always take care of you, Ty. Things are going to get better here, and your life will be different than it has been. I wish I could be here to see that."

Ty threw himself into Chase's arms. He laid his head on top of the boy's head, breathing in his scent. The comforting smells of syrup mixed with dirt filled his nostrils. The smells of youth. Leaning back, he ruffled the boy's hair.

"I'll miss you, Chase."

"I'll miss you, too, Ty."

CHAPTER 73

August 8th. 8:00am.

I think we are ready...

Alyx tested the zipper on her backpack one more time. Everything was packed. She paced the room. The two of them were alone in the house they had been living in since the victory against the hunters. They had agreed that this was the best place to exit this dimension, both for the sake of privacy and for the sake of keeping the secret of the watches.

She knew they had succeeded in this seventh dimension to the best of their abilities. Alyx had begun writing her own journal of the events that had transpired here, so there would be documentation for future keepers in her family. The one thing they hadn't done was search for the third watch and the next keeper. There just hadn't been time for that under the circumstances. If the third remaining keeper was in this dimension, they had failed that part of the mission.

"I think we can assume we will both jump to Dune Harbor. I just wish we could jump together to the same location."

"What if we hold hands? Anything we are wearing or holding goes with us, right? If we hold hands, maybe we'll end up in the same place."

She tilted her head. "True. We do take things with us each time we jump, but what if our touching throws everything off? Since this hasn't been done before, we have no idea if our two transports will be compatible, or if combining them will have disastrous consequences. We could end up anywhere, or worse, not survive the jump. Maybe we should just take our chances and hope to find each other quickly once we get there. Maybe make a meeting point?"

"Easy for you to say. You didn't have to see me die a horrible death. I don't want to risk something like that happening again, Alyx. I'd rather die together during the jump than lose you again."

She blew out a breath. "Okay. We'll try holding hands. But just in case that doesn't work, meet me at Uncle Charlie's house as soon as you can."

"Okay, if we don't arrive together, I'll see you at the house."

She looked at her watch. 8:05.

"Ready?"

"Ready."

They stood side-by-side, backpacks on, holding hands. Chase absently rubbed his thumb on the palm of Alyx's hand as they waited.

"Three minutes seems like an eternity when you are waiting."

"True."

8:07. Each of their watches began glowing brightly, as if in anticipation.

"Good luck, Chase."

"I love you, Alyx."

She inhaled a deep breath and looked into his glowing blue eyes. "I..."

All at once electricity filled the room, and both of their bodies hummed with power of it. Dual silver ever-changing pools appeared above each of their heads, seeming to take on a life of their own. When they emerged, they measured about the size of a quarter, hovering over each of them, and then grew before their eyes to the size of a full-length mirror in the blink of an eye. Their constantly changing shapes writhed in anticipation of the passing minute, as if barely able to contain the excitement of the moment, like a child running down the stairs on Christmas morning.

8:08.

Chase looked at Alyx questioningly. "What?"

"I..." Suddenly, she launched herself at Chase, wrapping her arms around him and holding on. He caught her, stumbling back a step, and returned her embrace, enfolding her in his arms and hugging her body to his. Again, their bodies fit perfectly together. His hard lines meshed with her soft curves. Alyx squeezed her eyes shut, her head tucked under Chase's chin, and waited.

A bolt of lightning streaked through the room as the two shimmering pools bounced off of each other like opposing magnetic forces. His blue glow joined with her purple glow, combining to create one deep mulberry color that ran through their veins and throughout both of their bodies, as if they had become one unit.

Anticipation turned to attack as the writhing pools above them continued to bounce off of each other, as if engaged in some kind of epic battle, until one final crash when, accompanied by another bolt of lightning, they united, creating one large mercurial silver pool above them.

The cosmic war ended abruptly, and they moved peacefully as one. Just a second after the separate entities united, the now single large mass enveloped both of them at once, from head to foot in a heartbeat, as they disappeared from their current location instantaneously. The house where they had been standing just seconds before was suddenly vacant, and the only trace that anyone had been there was the electrical hum and a faint burning smell left in their wake.

And that's when the pain began.

To Be Continued...

View other Black Rose Writing titles at www.blackrosewriting.com/books and use promo code **PRINT** to receive a **20% discount** when purchasing.

BLACK ROSE
writing™